JAY LOVES LUCY

JAY LOVES LUCY

Fiona Cooper

SERPENT'S
TAIL

Library of Congress Catalog Card Number: 90-64195

British Library Cataloguing in Publication Data
Cooper, Fiona *1955*
   Jay Loves Lucy
   I. Title
   823. 914[F]

   ISBN 1-85242-218-1

The right of Fiona Cooper to be identified as author of this work
has been asserted by her in accordance with the Copyright,
Designs and Patents Act 1988

Copyright © 1991 by Fiona Cooper

First published 1991 by
Serpent's Tail, 4 Blackstock Mews, London N4

Set in 10/13 pt Astor by AKM Associates Ltd, London

Printed on acid-free paper by
Nørhaven A/S, Viborg, Denmark

JAY LOVES LUCY

It was one prehistoric evening when a sunset to remember filled the sky with garlands and streamers of gold and rose. The Mammoth was lumbering home when she swung her head up and noticed the grand finale in the sky. She couldn't watch and walk at the same time so she stopped immediately. She loved to stand still gazing in wonder at the beauties of Nature. Sometimes she closed her eyes for hours so that she could think. Mammoths can't do two things at once and nothing thinks deeper and slower than a mammoth.

'It's a sunset made for mammoths!' she thought in a long blink, for the sun went down so gently she was transfixed.

When the last drop of light tipped over the horizon she found she couldn't move. She was up to her ankles in ice. Oh, well, she thought, mammoths are strong. She tugged at one great big hairy foot but it would not budge. As she bent her head to see what was happening, a slow chill curve of water sneaked across the ice and froze as it flowed.

Mammoths rage and stomp. This one could only raise her hairy trunk to the full cold moon and trumpet her pain while the water built icy layers up to her chest. Her last thought began as her heartbeat slowed to zero.

'And there was . . .'

By morning, there was only a dark shape shrouded in ice.

Maybe a million years later, the sun rose red and hot and the ice began to melt. The Mammoth's hairy great head emerged as the ice-block slipped lower and, after a while, her back. And when the frozen chains around her chest began to snap, her heart went boom! and out slipped the end of her thought:

'So much I wanted to do . . .'

She looked around, with a strong suspicion that something had been going on while she had her back turned. But to follow that thought would mean days of standing still with eyes tight shut and she felt she'd maybe been standing in one place far too long.

She was a bit stiff at first, and it took her a few days to limber up to the kind of tree-breaking lumber a mammoth does best. She had a ball, eating as if she was starved, swimming, stomping her happy hairy feet all over the place, feeling like she'd been born again.

But something peculiar had happened: she felt uneasy around sunsets. She couldn't remember why. Mammoths always forget, which explains why elephants are common even now. What was it about the evening sun going down? She loved to watch, but found herself shifting from one magnificent shaggy foot to another. It spoiled the experience; she couldn't concentrate. After a while, she stopped watching sunsets and felt a good deal easier though rather melancholy and for the life of her she couldn't think why. But she kept moving.

There came a day when she was loping home, thinking nothing in particular. She swung her head up and found herself transfixed by a grand finale sunset like she'd never seen before.

'It's a sunset made for mammoths!' she thought, for the sun sank almost imperceptibly, tossing veils of gold and lilac and rose around the sky like a beautiful dancer. The Mammoth's thirsty eyes drank it in.

The last drop of sun tipped over the horizon and she wanted to make her way home. Only she found she couldn't move her feet.

'Oh, dear,' said the Mammoth shaking her wonderfully woolly head, 'my feet appear to be freezing over.'

And then in the darkness, the chill water came welling up around her, and as the baleful moon swung up in the sky, she remembered the last time as clear as sheet ice. She raised her trunk to the stars in despair to cry her pain.

'It was so good to be unfrozen and feel alive again,' she thought, when she'd trumpeted herself hoarse. 'I didn't like freezing last time, especially when the cold reached my heart and I thought I was dying.'

'But it has been such a wonderful summer,' wailed the Mammoth. No one was listening. 'I have so enjoyed this summer, and why shouldn't a mammoth be warm?'

She still tried to shift her enormous feet, but the ice was set solid to the centre of the earth and all the Mammoth's tears froze as they fell. Furious and frantic, she started to think:

'I must never stop . . .'

And then she was frozen deep under the ice.

Another million years went by before the sun came out strong enough to melt the ice. Out came the Mammoth and out came the end of her thought.

' . . . dancing!' she trumpeted aloud.

And whether she ever froze again — who knows?

CHAPTER ONE

When I was one and twenty,
I heard a wise man say,
'Give crowns and pounds and guineas
But not your heart away . . .'

Mid-thirties and Jay was given to Falling In Love. She joked that it was her favourite occupation. Usually her passion was an explosion of ecstasy, at a face, a voice, a mannerism; usually she did nothing about it beyond engineering to spend time in The Presence. Doing anything more led to agony, sleepless nights, months of drinking and moping and boring her closest friends to death. Once bitten twice brashly armoured? Not Jay.

'I have been *savaged* by love,' she would declaim, when she'd had a few. 'But many years ago, a wise old man said fall in love and you may fall flat on your face, but pick yourself up and rush towards the next one, knees bleeding, face bruised, arms open, heart on fire.'

Dear Walter the art teacher, old-fashioned gallant, shouting 'bugger' in class, casting lofty pearls to the in-group of disaffected teenagers. She'd taken him literally, although now she questioned whether that had been wise.

Hollywood stars were safe to fall in love with, dead or a million dollars away. Tennis stars. People at bus stops. And Jay would bathe in a glow of wonder that another human being could move her so. After the first few devastating out-of-loves, she was warily certain that there would always be another goddess; the old idol became a fond memory, like a photo of a dear friend long absent. Once in love, always loving. Never letting go of that feeling, even when the flash-fire gut-lurch of In Love seemed distant, ludicrous, incredible. In Love again, the new beloved was perfect and miraculous; Jay swept away what she had learned in pain about feet of clay and natural caution. Her heart went into a cartoon clinch: *Nothing Else Matters*!

Lucy was different. Jay had felt fleeting sexual desire when they first met in the corridor where she worked, a tumbledown rats' nest in East London. A pleasant surprise so early in the day: Lucy had style, from well-cut red-gold hair down through the subtly tailored suit, to the jaunty tap-tap of grey suede sub-stilettoes. A designer dyke! She expected Lucy to head for their office: no one else was ever in before noon on the top floor. But Lucy smiled distractedly, passed her, leaving a scent of honeysuckle and spice. She unlocked the next room which had stood empty for months.

'We have neighbours,' she told Francis, her co-worker.

'Nice?' he drawled. 'Any trade?'

'A very respectable looking lady, dear,' she said, 'wearing a million dollar perfume.'

'Is that all? Mm. Better make her coffee, darling,' he said. 'You never know.'

Somehow among the chaos of coffee cups and a snowstorm of phonecalls and paper, she and Francis and a cheerfully unreliable string of volunteers threw together every month a gay arts magazine. A lot of women put her down for working with a man, especially one like Francis, camp as Christmas in Tangiers, a slow fuse of lasciviousness smouldered in every phrase. But he made her laugh and worked like hell for peanuts. His favourite topics were sex and sex and he hadn't repeated himself once in three years. Jay giggled along with him, they cried on each other's shoulders and, every week or so over cocktails, swore to marry each other.

She made coffee, flicked a V sign at Francis's suggestive tongue and knocked on Lucy's door.

The room was bare and filthy, an unfurnished twin to theirs. Raddled nets trailed at grey window-panes, flakes of plaster flecked the bare boards, newsprint, piss-yellow with age, scrunched at her feet. Lucy looked very small and determined and was making a list.

'Thought you'd like some coffee,' Jay said. 'This place is so bleak. I'm Jay. We're next door.'

'That's kind. I'm Lucy,' said Lucy.

'In fact, do come and have a seat,' said Jay.

'I think I will,' said Lucy, 'I didn't realise quite how bad it would be.'

'Francis, this is Lucy,' she said.

'Lovely to meet you, darling. Toss aside those master-pieces of illiteracy and have a chair,' he said. 'Welcome to pervert posers anonymous. What do *you* do?'

'We're an ecology magazine,' said Lucy. 'I edit. Can't write, can spell.'

'Oh, good!' said Francis from the heart. 'I'm ever so dyslexic, aren't I, dear? But I do have other talents. And I must pop out and get some milk. Want anything? No?'

He unfolded his incredibly long legs, arranged a white scarf at his throat and checked the mirror.

'I must re-do these highlights! Ta ta. Back soon unless I meet something *divine!*' He made an exit worthy of Noel Coward.

'What *do* you do?' said Lucy, guardedly, snapping a flame to the tip of a cigarette.

'Oh, Francis always says we're pervert posers' anonymous — we do an arts magazine, *Pink I Do Like*, gay and lesbian stuff. Have a look.'

'Oh,' said Lucy, clearly surprised to see glossy sophistication issue from such a down-market maelstrom. 'It's a good-looking product. My son's a painter.'

But not gay, thought Jay as Lucy blushed slightly. A son probably meant straight and married. The gold-ringed finger on her left hand confirmed it. A pin-striped husband in the city patronisingly fond of the little woman and her projects. And so on. Bad luck, Jay! She didn't feel up to a zealous dyke conversion. When in her twenties, nothing could stop her and she was proud to remember marriages faltering and once even, Astrid's, biting the dust.

Over the months Jay found she liked being around Lucy, enjoyed desiring her and doing nothing about it. It suited her easy-going semi-idleness. Lucy had the decency and zest of a boarding school prefect, the kind the Lower Third would swoon over. Jay was amused by her go-getting energy, especially when Lucy had done battle with yet another charitable trust or foundation. This verve, this ambition and Jay's laid-back curl of desire threw up a picture of Lucy as a B-movie dominatrix — but very, very civilised. Jay would nod and reply, make coffee, light cigarettes and smile at her silk stocking fantasy.

Lucy's clothes were impeccably respectable, the cut and cloth murmuring *I know I cost money, but there's no need to stare*. Good careful jewellery – usually she sported a gold looped cameo at her throat, very conventional, but with the cream wisped relief of a voluptuous woman naked against the nipple-pink shell. Over coffee in the office, in the middle of a serious conversation, Lucy would edge her shoes off, stretch her feet and say:

'Bloody tart-trotters. Still, it impresses the grant-givers, without whom . . .'

Each business meeting put a spark of challenge in her green eyes. She led with the chin and got her own way most of the time. Francis would snort with laughter when she and her natty briefcase had left in White Rabbit haste.

'Lovely legs, darling, aren't you tempted? And the heaven-sent heaven scent!'

'I'm settling into comfortable middle age, Francis. Me and a few short stories. I've done my running around.'

She and Lucy would have a drink after work on Fridays, sometimes an early supper, a few hours to unwind: a pattern pleasing to both. Over the years, over coffee, lunch, drinks now and then, she found out more: yes to straight, yes to married, but divorced for some fifteen years. Lucy's son was the apple of her eye, work her raison d'être. She had a passion for fine music and fine art. She was much more fun after a few drinks, gently mocking her dedication to saving this planet. Around the third glass of wine, she would become vehement, a soft rose rising to her cheeks from the ivory-silk of her blouse. Then she sparkled, took a ritzy walk to the bar and could be delightfully and surprisingly coarse. She worked from eight till late, even in winter. And she got things done: two days after she moved in, the place was 'positively sanforised, dear,' said Francis, wall-to-wall carpeting, curtains from Heals', furniture in place, phones installed and busy. Lucy.

Jay's fleeting lust metamorphosed — practically —

into interest and friendship; sometimes on the way home, lyrically drunk and alone, she would fantasise about kissing Lucy, stroking the fine lines etched around her eyes and on her brow, nuzzling into her throat and shoulders. . . . She had to smile when the busy reality met her the following day.

CHAPTER TWO

Lucy worried about her son and drugs, her son and girls, her son and money. My son, my son. Her eyes plunged to a russet flecked deep green when she talked about him. Gradually she confided in Jay who was happy to listen and soothe. Flattered, even, that someone so utterly different and reserved had opened up to her, late-thirties dyke pottering around to nowhere.

'Time for a drink?' Lucy, airily around their door.

Jay always had time for a drink.

'Are you coming, Francis?'

'I think it's girls' talk,' said he, archly.

'Oh, piss off, you silly old queen. It's more like Claire Rayner!'

'But you love it, darling!'

'It's all right,' said Jay, grinning absurdly. It was pleasant to feel needed by an attractive older woman, it amused her when Lucy pecked her goodbye. Always brisk, always on the cheek. Food for fantasy.

It was springtime when she fell in love with Lucy. On St Patrick's Day, at 7.48 in the evening, just like that. She clutched at these landmarks as her heart soared like a kite, time day and place an anchor to the swooping flight of love.

Lucy had asked her to supper in her West London flat. She wanted to co-ordinate an article about trees and pollution and Jay and Francis had discovered a photographer who only did trees and did them brilliantly. Jay was knocked out by his work, Francis ecstatic over his tight torn jeans, and Lucy's eyes lit up when she saw the portfolio.

'Oh, you can have all the blight and disease, dear,' Francis told her, 'we'll stick with the sunshine and thrusting buds. All things bright and beautiful,' he trilled. 'Sorry, couldn't resist!'

Lucy wanted Jay to help her write the article. Jay was delighted with the compliment and intrigued to see inside Lucy's flat. Oh horseshit, Jay! When Lucy asked her, her fantasy took a careful half-step forwards. Dinner was not lunch, and an evening was the prelude to night. *Thank you*, she said, *I'd love to*. She ignored Francis's frankly suggestive eyebrows — damn him for knowing her!

'Well, dear!' he said. 'You've got a date. Bit serious tho'. And you! Miss Never-do-a-minute-of-overtime! A working date!'

'Life is not all lust,' said Jay, swatting him.

'Mind my rollers, dear! No, you have to sleep sometime,' he said.

The day before the date, Jay went into Lucy's office and saw her crying, silky red head on the desk, fists clenched. Wanted to put her arm around her, hug her, what the hell had super-brat been up to now? She tiptoed out unnoticed. Later Lucy borrowed coffee, a picture of composure. Jay was intrigued, but knew better than to ask the question direct. Vinegar on a clam, that. And Lucy said:

'Got to get back early this evening. Can't stop for a drink. But I'm seeing you tomorrow, anyway, aren't I? Seven-thirty? Bye.'

'Oui, mon capitaine!' giggled Francis. 'You've got your orders. Come and have a Slow Comfortable Screw Against the Wall with an ageing deviant. It's a cocktail, dear.'

'I know what a slow comfortable screw is, Francis,' said Jay in her best Mae West, 'but I ain't never done it against a wall.'

'Very wise,' said he.

That night Jay dreamed in glorious technicolour with full Dolby stereo.

Lucy was weeping as she had been that afternoon. But Jay did not tiptoe away. Late afternoon sun spilled white shafts across the desk to light her hair with a jewelled sheen the colour of pomegranates. Jay drifted through the dazzle to hold her, kissed her agonisingly soft hair, breathed her perfume, kissed her closed wet eyes with a tenderness that stabbed through her with a sword of fire.

And then she was driving through a heliotrope dusk, a summer evening in deep country lanes, green trunks leopard shadowed, a billion emerald leaves overhead greying as she drove. Lucy was beside her, smiling and weary. No words. But all the sweet and strange scents of evening, the chill of night. And the Pergolese largo enhancing the enchanted dusk with sparse fluidity, unearthly serenity, *When I behold the body* . . .

And Lucy. Now holding her hand like a shy and trusting child.

They were in the foyer of a country hotel. Signing a book. And walking together on thick-carpeted stairs, hand trailing a blackened balustrade, beams in the ceiling. Their room. White ceiling, white curtains shifting in a breeze, a huge bed neither would admit they had seen and what it meant.

And so the dining room. A real log fire. Jay drank a smoky oak ruby wine. Lucy filled her glass with the palest gold, firelight making a star in the bowl, the label on the wine was olive-green and gold and Lucy's eyes were spring leaves dancing in the light of dawn.

They had come to the hotel to make love. Lucy was shy as hell, and Jay was sure and easy. O my beloved! They talked about everything but, mouths moving and laughing with no sound: Jay saw them now as if on film, now from inside her thrilling flesh, looking at Lucy, making her laugh, feeling the thick cream linen napkin, the solid edge of the table.

And Lucy knew they were there to be lovers, Jay knew like her heartbeat that they would make love. In their room the lights were honey-pale, and Lucy turned away to undress. But Jay sat on the bed, she had brought brandy liqueur and crystal glasses. My love, my dove, my life, I love you! Oh, the mandarin old gold. Lucy's lips tasted of brandy, their first kiss. No words, just the blissful caress of cool cotton sheets as they slid into bed, Jay's body glowing with desire. And Lucy's silky warm skin all along her, arms wrapped round each other, so close that nothing could come between.

So close that Jay didn't know where she ended and Lucy began. She cupped her hands round Lucy's sweet fine chin and drew her lips against her own, tongue trembling into the wet hotness of Lucy's mouth, exploring behind her lips, Lucy's tongue tentative then sure. She lay safe, held warm, and Jay drew adoring fingertips along her throat, learning her ear lobes by heart, Lucy's breast was so soft and smooth, Jay dipped her head and sucked her nipple, in ecstasy, in prayer, fingers tracing mystery. A baby had been here, this close . . . Her hand moved ahead of her lips, ablaze when she brushed the fine wiry hair between Lucy's thighs, all at once a mapless explorer in a rich forest.

And her blind fingertips sought the sweet elusive bud of ecstasy, her mouth followed blindly, lips meeting their own dizzy baptism. Above her, below her, inside her, her being welded to Lucy, Lucy. Lucy all around. Lucy's body shuddered, oceans of sweat bound them, tide-tossed, tempest-tossed, redeemed.

Like all new lovers they made love all night, laughed, stopped for a cigarette whose smoke tantalised in the lazy glow of the room. They slept in the first grey twitterings of dawn, Jay tore herself away to hang the prosaic Do Not Disturb sign on the door. Nothing could disturb this love. Then back to the exhausted heat of Lucy, and sleep. Sleep.

Sun through the curtains, she woke with Lucy in her arms. Sleep, my darling. She woke Lucy with coffee, and more loving, sure and slow. Now she knew how to tease and tantalise her, hold her on the brim of honeydew euphoria then flood her wordless yearning with a Niagara of delirium.

Driving home, dropping Lucy a block from her life, her house, her son. And knowing this was just a beginning.

Jay woke early, and turned to hold Lucy. Jesus! The dream drifted away, and for once she had pen and paper, made a cigarette and wrote until the alarm went off. It was a story, it flowed.

It was a love letter, it was what she wanted and would she have the nerve to deliver it? Could she? Could she not?

CHAPTER THREE

Jay had not fallen in love very often. Well, apart from that camp every other day thrill . . . But seldom with anything approaching seriousness. Flirting and charming, usually home alone and no regrets next day. She had worked like hell at getting people to like her, believing herself gross and hideous as a child.

'Sarah's pretty,' said her mother, awarding first prize to her sister. 'You've got personality.'

Jay's mother managed to slide a moral judgement or evaluation into every statement. Pretty meant vacuous, personality meant show-off, having fun was shopgirl mentality. She had ill-equipped both daughters for life, disapproving of fashion and make-up, deaf to music both classical and popular. In fact what the hell had she enjoyed? Her garden and going to church? Jay couldn't think of anything else.

Her mother had both children late in life, and was wonderful for the first six years of Jay's life. Jay remembered the sun in the garden, the paddling pool, her mother meeting her after school, face lighting up with love and joy as her little girl pelted out of school like a tornado, seized her mother's hand and dragged her home down the street, read to her, played with her, woke her with a kiss, read her a bedtime story. Happy days!

But it had all soured later. When she was ten? Eleven? Her mother's moodswings began to terrify her, and she would slow to a careful frozen walk as she turned into their street. If there was a car outside the house, she relaxed and speeded up: a car meant visitors and her mother charming, not mad and spiteful.

She was a teenager in the sixties. Too young and protected to go to festivals, she grew her hair long like John Lennon and loved John Lennon after Yoko because he too wore glasses but didn't care. Also her parents hated John and Yoko, switching off *Top of the Pops*, saying they were sacrilegious: *Christ, you know it ain't easy!* became her silent song. Her sister listened to

The Moody Blues, Jay listened to Bob Dylan, Joan Baez, The Kinks: she despised the early, clean-cut Beatles and mods. In the town there were mods and rockers, leather-clad and terrifyingly male, or smart, self-assured and terrifyingly male.

She adored greasers, saw a motorbike as a symbol of freedom: just climb on and go. Go. Go. Go to Woodstock, the sea, the top of a mountain, a river, go forever from the flat respectability of home and market town. Jay tie-dyed shirts purple with white star bursts, stopped wearing shoes, wore fringed waistcoats, Indian head-bands, bought incense and cultivated a dead-pan expression. She didn't look like she was there; she knew she didn't want to be there. She thought she was ugly and monstrously fat, and was always surprised and cynical when boys/men talked to her. One of the going-steady girly types at her school told her boys thought she was cool and superior. This made her cry desperately. She was sure they didn't really like her, it hadn't occurred to her that she might be off-putting. The first time a boy kissed her, she thought he was being charitable and told him he didn't have to. Could not believe he really wanted to.

But Woodstock and the sunshine hippies broke through the clouds of small-town standards, and Jay scoured the Oxfam shop for silk and satin and velvet. She hung around in their sub-hippy world, camou-flaged, but never feeling she belonged.

There were exceptions. John for example. John van Loon. John van Loon had been sent home from work for wearing a kaftan and he laughed about it. He told her she had a lovely body and when she went to bed with him, she said (he'd find out about it anyway and drop her):

'I have a confession to make.'

He held her close.

'I have spots on my back. It's embarrassing.'

'Oh dear,' he said, kissing her. 'Well, I have something to tell you, too.'

God! he hadn't thrown her out.

'My little man goes red when I'm excited.'

Someone else bothered by their body? A man? News to Jay. She fucked him with enthusiasm, they laughed, they did it again and again — on and off for years. She liked him, never thought of him as a boyfriend, he was too comfortable. Actually, she could probably have married him and had a few nice babies with his laughing blue eyes, his loony hippy fluffy hair, and maybe her eyebrows. Jay liked her eyebrows, straight and black but with a decided curve at the end. That was the one part of her body she liked, and with her glasses they were masked. She was blind as an owl in daylight without glasses: therefore nothing to look at. Three wishes would have brought her perfect sight, a million pounds and an ape-hanger motorbike.

So. The ten commandments of her teenage.

All you need is love. (I am unlovable.)

The old order is rapidly changing. (I live in a town which has stayed the same for a thousand years beyond skirt-lengths and cars.)

You're beautiful, a child of the Universe. (I'm hideous, and a bad bad girl.)

You may not be here tomorrow. Do it today. (He comes like a Thief in the night, Christ, that is, and woe betide you if he finds you wanting.)

Thou shalt do everything that the church says thou shalt not. (But if it's true, said Jay's demons and nightmares, what if it's true? There's no hell, but I'm going there anyway ...)

If it feels good, do it. (Nothing feels particularly good. Calm down, cheer up, control your temper, wipe that make-up off, you look like a tart, look at the way you walk, don't wear those trousers, put a dress on, men can't control themselves, it's up to you to take control, love bites are a sign of a man out of control, your sister's a tart, if you lose your name no one will have you, who do you think you are, listen to her — social life? While you're at school, my girl? You're getting some very odd ideas.)

Property is theft. (I should be saving, says my father.)

You must please men and be good in bed. (A decent man wants to marry a virgin.)

Men never make passes at girls who wear glasses. (I am blind as a bat without and contact lenses are too expensive and who do you think you are, you should be studying.)

Believe in yourself. (We should have had boys!)

We may not be here tomorrow screamed the rock-fuck bands. (Sufficient unto each day the evil thereof.)

Sins of the flesh? She was raped at thirteen and had an orgasm, her first. So she'd enjoyed it? Probably provoked it. Probably had VD. She masturbated. A lot. Didn't want to pass on what she'd got. And there was no one to tell. When she finally screamed it out at her mother four years later, her mother said:

'Don't go round telling everyone. It's nothing to be proud of it. It won't make you look important.'

CHAPTER FOUR

The office was empty when Jay got in, and she slid her dream onto her desk with a work folder to hide it from Francis's camp curiosity. With her mind wide open to this new enticing prospect, a desire so unexpected and untested, she wanted no audience. It was wonderful to feel again, to let herself go with it, to water-ski blindfold, to jump out of a plane and take a chance on the ripcord. Way to go! And Francis would know something was happening: he would not leave it be until he'd extracted every detail, he never did. But he rang at 10.30, hung over and apologetic. He would not be in at all if she could stand it. Jay grinned ear to ear, commiserated and ordered him back to bed.

The day was hers. She cleared her desk onto the floor, made coffee and switched on the typewriter. All the time was hers to work through her story/ fantasy(?)/love letter. After all these years of knowing Lucy, too! Her whole body felt starry-eyed and jubilant. She snapped Satie into the cassette and re-read what the night had brought her. Christ, it was explicit! Explicit? she mocked herself, yeah and why ever not? But a remnant of caution urged that she tone it down, after all, Lucy . . .

She began.

I first met you . . .

Four pages later she lit a cigarette. Hmm. Hedging. She hadn't even touched the dream. Then she decided to leave it. You don't mess with El Dorado. The four pages were an introduction, a portrait. And she typed the dream exactly as it had come to her. No way she could show this to Lucy! She felt a thrill in her gut. She did routine office stuff for the rest of the day, and only re-read it at five. She swaggered out of the door like a Mississippi gambler.

Maybe.

Home, a bath, a mere-smear of slap and fresh clothes. She put her bag with the story on the passenger seat and drove as if it were a newborn baby. At traffic lights she gave it a wary smile, slid into gear and played Nina Simone's 'I need a Little Sugar in My Bowl'. She had decided this was the theme, exactly what Lucy needed, locked in work and the vagaries of her maverick genius boy-child.

The car flew up onto the Westway.

She pictured Lucy. Would she dare to challenge that tight-jawed efficiency with a declaration of passion? Dedicated to the one I love?

Drive, you ridiculous bitch!

Jay adored the Westway, swooping over a London bright as Woolworth's jewellery counter, streetlight brilliants and flyover neon like topaz on a chain; red and green and amber a flashing diamond ... It was the flight path the one man she'd ever been In Love with had taken her for the first time, after a late film at the Paris Pullman, Kensington to Hampstead at two a.m. She'd never let go of him, either, even when their affair was over, and he was tramping the globe looking for Nirvana. Every six months, she'd ring him and listen to the ravings of his latest guru. Then he'd inherited and blown the lot, only alcoholism and smack-addiction to show for it after eighteen months. She'd seen him many times then, everyone else had dropped him, and only moneyed privilege had kept him out of the gutter. It had made her feel like a dutiful grown-up daughter, visiting a hypochondriac distant relative once a week.

Finally his double-barrelled family had stepped in and bought the prodigal a mega-mineral cure and a pent-house flat. At which point she unlocked her ball and chain. She hadn't seen him in seven years and didn't really want to.

Now she was near the Lucy exit. And the lights were green. Jay took such things as an omen. If there was cherry blossom in Lucy's street, she'd show her treasure! At least that was a decision.

She stopped at an off-licence and recklessly bought pink champagne. If her love-letter was the Titanic, let it go down glorious, awash with roses, evening dress and a decadent late-night piano playing 'Them There Eyes'. Ha! She drove down the wide west London avenue. On the street where Lucy lived, cherry trees were bursting with pink and white like fairground popcorn. She parked, suddenly chill, picked up her bag as if it held eggshells. Well, well . . .

Her fantasy hit the earth as Lucy in the flesh opened the door. She had changed since work, to black tailored trousers and a cashmere sweater of black and Irish green.

'Brought some wine,' said Jay. 'Self-indulgence. Pink champagne, my favourite. Hope you like it.'

'I've never had pink champagne,' said Lucy.

What? Jay raged against the divorced husband and all the lovers Lucy was sure to have had in between. Why, this woman should have bathed in pink cham-pagne. Already, Jay's Hollywood imagination was building her beds of rose-petals under crystal minarets. Steady, she told herself, we are here to work. Lucy's self-contained sophistication sipped at the ultimately silly drink. Champagne had brought Ninotchka to her feet, declaiming, *I vant to make a speech!* Garbo laughs! Jay sipped and etched Lucy's face and gestures on her mind, in the rose-pink glow of having seen her weeping and helpless, thinking she was alone. But I am here with you! Jay made a reckless pledge, feeling ianthine waves lap her limbs into a sure promise of ecstasy.

Lucy cooked pasta, Jay could hardly eat, and lit a cigarette as soon as decently possible. Smoke curled, wine flowed, and Lucy put her fabulous legs on a chair, smoking too, the most relaxed thing Jay had ever seen her do.

'You write,' said Lucy.

Jay blushed, the story in her bag radio-active fluorescence. Yeah, lady, I write. I also want to rip your clothes off and appreciate you like you've never known.

'I've never been able to,' said Lucy. 'I can foster talent: look at my son, Jeremy.'

The walls were hung with competent oils. Clever, even.

'He's good,' Jay allowed. 'I've brought you a story.'

Aw, shit, momma! she protested, you've done it now.

'I'd love to read it,' said Lucy, good child that she was.

'Um, it's a bit personal,' said Jay, stalling, suddenly fascinated by the floor tiles.

Lucy laughed: Jay thought of medieval tapestries and silver hunting horns. She mammoth walked to her bag and removed the offending sheets. *It's now or never*, thrummed her jukebox memory, unbidden. She selected the first three pages — Lucy as she'd been allowed to see her, and handed them over. Lucy read, and between her sudden fascination for the floor tiles, edge of the table cloth, light thru' the wine glasses, Jay shot glances at Lucy, delirious at how small her hands were, how the rings she wore seemed to hold those tiny fingers together, how she longed to touch, kiss and suck those hands, nuzzle the inside of Lucy's wrists.

Lucy looked up when she had finished reading.

'And?' Jay said, her eyes questing.

She poured more champagne and noticed her hands were shaking. She drew on her cigarette.

'And,' she said drily, casting the purple passages over the table like a deck of cards. Eat your heart out, Diamond Jim Brady! What the hell. She focused on the rim of her wine glass as phrases from the story danced mockingly across her memory. *You've done it now,* she thought, numbing herself against Lucy's inevitable knowing look and dismissive laugh.

But Lucy did not laugh. Was shaking, in fact, as she put the pages on the table between them. A silence.

'God,' she said, not looking at her. 'You do know how to make love.'

'Sorry dear,' said Jay. 'Just couldn't resist. Look, laugh it off, forget it, sorry.'

'I'd never laugh at this,' said Lucy. 'I don't know what to say.'

This Jay had not expected. A fling, a flingette, a sophisticated snigger. But Lucy pale and unable to meet her eyes? Jay floundered.

'How does it feel to have a dyke fancy you rotten?' she managed.

'Strange,' said Lucy, 'very strange. I really don't know what to say.'

'I must go to the loo,' said Jay.

'Jay — what do you *want*?' said Lucy as Jay dived upstairs on the tide of a blush.

'YOU!' Jay called, slamming the loo door. Her heart pounded as she peed. Whatever next? She zipped her jeans and sauntered back downstairs to the other side of the table from Lucy. Cool it, she ordered her imminent coronary, cool it. But Lucy had moved to an easy chair and sat, chin cupped by an exquisite palm. Jay penned her in, one hand on each arm rest and kissed her neck. So bold! She sat in the opposite chair while Lucy put a record on; she flung one leg across the other knee, rolled a cigarette and contained the volcano surging from her clitoris to tight silent lips.

'We should do some work,' said Lucy.

But Jay's spine became electric as Pergolese's *Stabat Mater* came through the speakers sure as it had filled the dusk of her dream. The only logical conclusion was that they should go to bed.

Lucy arranged the contents of a folder on the table and set up a typewriter. Jay wrenched herself into the present.

They sat side by side. 'You type,' said Lucy. Ideas flew from Lucy's lips, Jay worked them into the right phrase, the right anaology. And all at once, it was midnight.

'I'm shattered,' said Lucy.

'Tough shit,' said Jay. 'Let's get the damn thing finished.'

'Now?' said Lucy.

'Yeah, now,' said Jay, grinning. 'You didn't know how hard I can work, did you? But only when I really want to. Like writing. Like making love.'

Right on time! Enter the beloved son. Tall, lazily handsome, and boy did he know it! Jay resented him immediately, and immediately told herself not to be stupid. But he had just slid his key into the lock, simply strolled in and shattered their precious time. He smiled and yawned. Lucy leapt up at once. *Hello, darling*! All her time and mind alert for him.

'Hi, mum. Oh, you're Jay? Hi. I'm Jem.'

You would be, snarled Jay, smiling back and lighting a cigarette.

Lucy stretched up to peck his cheek, and he patted her as if conferring an honour.

'Have you eaten?' said Lucy, half-way to the table.

'Too tired, mum. Don't fuss. I'm dead! Goodnight!'

He loped upstairs two steps at a time. A door closed, taps ran, the loo flushed. Another door closed, then silence. He lived here all right. He took it all for granted, and would never have a clue just how blessed he was.

Jay rushed through the rest of the article. They moved across to easy chairs. Lucy poured brandy. It felt to Jay like her time was very nearly up. And shouldn't Lucy say *something* about her story, the subtle and extravagant passes Jay had been making at her all evening? Something should *happen*!

Suddenly there was silence. Cool it, Jay! she told herself, this is all very new. And Lucy was perfectly capable of saying *do stay the night.*

She didn't. There was a shy tense hug and lip brush of a kiss at the door. Enough to have Jay fly home on the wings of Peter Pan and sleep like an angel. Now she knew where Lucy lived and Lucy knew how she felt. Just in case there was any doubt about it, she decided the woman needed flowers every day, and she would be the one to send them.

Lucy was not at work the next day, Francis was writhing in voyeuristic anticipation, Jay was mute, and Access and Interflora were making easy money.

Lucy rang her in the evening.

'Thank you for the flowers,' she said, with blackbird song precision. 'There was really no need — I realised I had a sweet and cheeses, you must have been starving.'

Do I need a sweet and cheeses when I can feed on your face? thought Jay. She said:

'I was fine, fine. Said a lot of things I've been meaning to for a long time.'

A pause. The lines humming, Jay wordless.

Chit-chat, chit-chat, and see you tomorrow.

Night and a bottle of hot-blooded Spanish wine brought a poem to Jay, the first one for years. She looked at it and could see no fault; she thought of Lucy and didn't care. My heart, my life. I love you!

Lucy was her immaculate self at work in the morning; they had a drink in the pub, and it was as if that evening, the story, the kiss, the flowers, had not been. But late night Jay tore into the poem, words flowing like wine from an oak cask, and — what the hell? — redeemed by the dawn spring of Lucy's eyes, she put the poem in an envelope, avoided Francis's deep meaningful questions: this love had no confidantes, not even one as well known and sweet as he.

CHAPTER FIVE

Lucy did not refer to that evening or to the story. But there was something in the air like hummingbirds poised over exotic blooms or velvet sheened butterflies. Jay found Lucy's eyes on her sometimes when she looked up, but there was little enough time to meet. A plan occurred to her; she and Lucy would go away for a weekend to the heart of the country, roses round the door, and find out how they would be lovers. If . . .

Her dreams were so vivid while the poem shimmered on her desk — signed, sealed, undelivered — that she had to catch herself from grabbing Lucy's hands, kissing her right out in the street, holding her close at the end of each day, saying, come home, darling; grabbing her and flinging her to the floor, ripping her clothes off, sinking into her breasts, fucking her like a sheet of flame. There was time enough for that . . . later.

And then she decided, one Lucyless evening of Marvin Gaye and Millie Jackson, *Come Live With Me*

Angel, I wanna kiss you all over — she decided to send the poem. This was year one, everything was a world premiere.

'Voilà,' she thought, tossing the letter into the postbox, 'Ma vie est faite.'

It was near midnight. The first post went at 7.30 a.m. The poem would arrive in two days' time. She checked her diary. What? The day after tomorrow she was actually going to be with Lucy at a conference on ecology and the arts. They'd arranged it months ago. Francis had raised an eyebrow at her enthusiasm. Jay never went to conferences, but as she accepted a lift with Lucy, he smiled with open pleasure.

'You outrageous dyke, you're just oozing with lust!' he said. 'I love that.'

'So do I,' said Jay. 'Just hope she does.'

'How can she not?' said Francis. 'Have fun, darling.'

Well, it wasn't an oak-beamed house in the hills, but it was some way out of the city. Jay's mind and body looped their loop.

Lucy drove, deft competent hands guiding them through the suburbs, Jay lit cigarettes for them both, a secret kiss at the tip of each one; houses blurred past beyond Lucy's profile. And soon it was trees, and then they parked. Paused.

'Did you get your poem?' said Jay biting her tongue.

'Yes,' said Lucy, awkwardly.

'You are my inspiration,' said Jay smiling, feeling easy, wanting Lucy to feel easy.

'Well it's a strange feeling to be someone's inspiration,' said Lucy. 'I'm glad if it helps.'

'I love you,' said Jay, very softly.

Lucy smiled a small tight-fisted smile. They registered at the desk.

Fool, clumsy fool! Why can't you wait? Can't you ever WAIT? Why do you always demand? She decided to do nothing else by way of wooing Lucy until there was real time, time for them to be alone. Together. She set her things round the monastic student bedroom.

CHAPTER SIX

One of Jay's drawled phrases, as she pubbed and clubbed and waded through hung-over mornings of coffee and endless cigarettes, was *I'm a night-owl, honey.'* Any conference she'd been to, everyone wound up in her room long after midnight, playing poker and spouting Bacardi bullshit, wine-bottle wisdom. But this weekend, her sure-fire heartbeat demanded that she spend every moment possible with Lucy. And the first evening in the bar, Lucy said she liked to rise early and walk, it was so rare and precious to be in the green and open air.

'Well, let's go for a walk,' said Jay. 'Tomorrow morning?'

'Seven o'clock?' said Lucy. 'It means we can skip breakfast. I always eat too much at conferences.'

Is there a seven o'clock in the morning? Curiouser and curiouser, Jay relished the idea: a new day in this new galaxy. And so she rose at six and bathed, tapped on Lucy's door at seven, to a clear ringing 'Come in!'

Lucy was as lovely first thing as always. *You'd be so nice to wake up with* . . . She rubbed on face cream, grimaced at her adorable lines and so together through the fields in the morning-o! It was the first blush after dawn, a fledgling day . . . Of course, Lucy was a runner, Jay a moocher, drinking in the mist and the birds and the rising chill. They left the conference building behind them. She had this absurd desire to swing Lucy round like a child and walk holding her hand. Instead she smiled with pioneer delight. Maybe, maybe, maybe!

Over the fields of the university campus, and a sudden low redbrick wall, a precisely colonnaded rose garden. Lucy spoke of her life, Jay wanted to hold her and hug the hurt away. Dew sat prettily on the roses, and they walked more slowly, Lucy looking at roses, Jay wishing she had a camera, knowing that, whatever else, now she was happy.

There was a conservatory too, a solid Victorian steam-palace of dark leaves and shaggy trunks towering like film scenery above them. They parted, and Jay watched Lucy through the fronds, utterly thrilled. Hey presto! a magic mauve flower at her feet, a reason to go to Lucy, touch her arm, say come here I want to show you something. Lucy came — Jay's fingertips blazoned with the feel of her warm flesh — and crouched to see. Her dear sweet silky head was a breath from Jay's lips, but Jay sensed in her a wild creature that scares easily, and held her tongue, her lips, her sanctified body, in check. Not now.

Back at the building, they parted. Jay lay on her bed, sipping coffee and touching her own face with the tenderness she felt for Lucy, closed her eyes with the dizzy perfection of that moment in the conservatory when they had touched, when she had touched Lucy, and Lucy had walked beside her, seen what she saw; when her eyes had met Jay's, dancing with the glory of it all.

CHAPTER SEVEN

A laser of moonrise stirred on Jay's pillow. She turned half-asleep in her big warm bed to curl an arm and herself round Lucy's hot soft body. Then woke to the empty pillow beside hers; body stretched in delicious ecstasy, as if her sweet saint had just that second ghosted away. Three-twenty, hours and hours to sleep and dream. She folded her arms round the pillow and murmured it and herself to sleep.

Dawn brought her a poem about starlight, Lucy's eyes. A poem for Lucy was a message in a bottle hurled into a turquoise ocean. Lucy had made it clear, if only by silence, that talk of love panicked her. Better to write, keep up a warm gentle insistent flow of words and wonderful cards. Jay would not be shut out and from what she could tell, Lucy didn't want to shut her out. Just keep the door on the latch. A tantalising maybe.

Jay felt she had been too long alone on her pure-white sandy desert island. She said she was no good at relationships — too hot, too cool, too frantic, too laid back, too jealous, too free. She'd given up and love had not visited her lonely shore in years. Her island was peopled with plumed parrots, preening dodos, psychedelic land crabs. Jay sought glitter, brassy jazz orchids of sensation, spectacle. Her island had a twenty-foot movie screen, a pantomime parade, carnival. Her friends came to visit in garish canoes, landed and partied and paddled home in the purple sunrise. Jay loved her friends.

But Lucy was a white-sailed trim-rigged yacht whose clean lines cut the waves straight to Jay's heart. And what a rich cargo she bore! A treasure-trove of forty something years of elegant piracy — Mexican silver, abalone, crystal, Schubert. There was a moon-glow about her, from her searching green eyes flickering with bronze to soft red-gold hair; her soul was elusive thistledown drifting in a moonbeam.

She is a unicorn, thought Jay, contriving ways to have their paths cross. A hermit crab sticks sand and weed on its shell, and all Jay's glitz was camouflage. She began to shed the brilliant borrowed chameleon plumage, she wanted to let Lucy in.

She started on her flesh. Jay was a solid woman, dressed in dark loose comfortable clothes that hid a multitude of sins. All at once she had to notch her belt tighter, found she had hipbones, cheekbones, found her breasts were round and firm. She bought scarlet jeans and loud shirts, shoes with rainbows on the toe. Love lit her from within and the light dancing from Lucy's radiant being brought her dancing to life.

She was so sure that time would change Lucy's fear of loving her that every unanswered poem spurred her on to something finer.

Those were the good days.

Bad days she reached for the neck of the nearest bottle, never quite drunk, never quite sober, maundering on to Francis about the impossibility of love. Francis, who knew Lucy, said little; Francis, who cared about Jay, kept brandy in the office. He kept clear when Lucy called in, kept his mouth shut unless Jay demanded his wisdom, advice that she would never take.

'Darling, you're spending a bloody fortune over this one. All for the privilege of a little pussybumping! You wish to insert your tongue into her vagina, and why not, you're both lovely. But this is turning into grand opera, dear, rehearsals at La Scala for *Götterdämmerung*...I hope she's worth it.'

'She is,' said Jay boring Francis sick with a detailed analysis of the last conversation she'd had with Lucy.

'Well, you are looking pretty good. If I were you I'd schlepp down to the disco and get yourself some trade, dear, otherwise you'll burst!'

Jay felt like an athlete in training: Lucy's perfection — and so her need for Jay's perfection to love her? — was her racetrack. This tingling *alive alive-o!*— Love — was her rigorous coach.

Time with Lucy was simply not enough. Jay had never been promiscuous after the fuck 'em and leave 'em college years, and now, after five years of no sex except occasional pleasant nights with ex-lovers, her newly spare body thrilled with anticipation. So a handclasp burned along her nerves and home again with just herself and music, she burned through sonnets sober as never before and high as a condor.

Maybe they had time alone once a week. And that time might just be a drink or a coffee — as always. But now, in her need. she noticed every moment with Lucy, pictured her, listened to the memory of her voice. The time they shared became special now, where before they had been free and easy. Love added uncertainty, love lavished all her extravagant colours and textures.

The day before Jay's birthday, Lucy said, 'Let's go somewhere different — Islington. Follow me.'

Jay's car was twenty years old and useless for long journeys. But nose to bumper she followed Lucy's city runabout and it was fine. She followed, and Lucy waved at her in the mirror at every light. Goddam, baby, you are something else! Jay was Bogart, Dietrich, even Anne Bancroft as her heart tugged along in Lucy's wake. They parked on adjacent meters. Both broken, alleluia! Jay walked in the frictionless sphere of one whom the gods have chosen.

But the café, Lucy's chosen place, was crowded and they had to share a table with the two cream blondes of the ski-tan variety, orange lipsticked, clad in cashmere.

'You know Peter?' said one.

'God, yah, Peter! Hard work!' said the other intensely.

Then their blonde heads met over a whisper, followed by twin ricochets of studied laughter.

'No!'

'Darling, I promise you!'

'My husband used to bring me here,' said Lucy quietly.

Jay wanted to know more of this husband, wonder boy's father, Lucy's one-time lover. His name was Martin and what had happened that he had let Lucy go? She never probed Lucy, fearful that she might withdraw. But a casual um or oh? a discreet sloshing of more wine would bring pink to Lucy's cheeks and untie her tongue. And at these times, she could hold Lucy's hand, and would melt when the pressure was returned.

'Oh?' said Jay, like who-gives-a-damn.

'Yes. If we'd had a row. To calm us down, get us out of the house. Rooms jangle after rows and no one could argue like me and Martin! Then suddenly we'd have to laugh, you know? There we would be, pistols at dawn and I'd laugh or he'd laugh and it would all be over. So we'd make our peace here.'

'Did you come here a lot?' said Jay, neutrally.

'Yes. We argued a lot. That table's free.'

They moved to relative privacy.

'So it's your birthday tomorrow,' said Lucy. Jay had asked her over to show her off to her four oldest friends.

'Yeah,' said Jay. 'One year nearer the big four O.'

'I remember it well,' said Lucy, grinning, 'OK, what do you want? For your birthday.'

For once, Jay was utterly rehearsed. She knew damn well what she wanted — Lucy stark naked and randy as hell. Hm. Lucy knew that too.

'I want a photo of you,' she said wolfishly, leaning back and smiling straight into Lucy's eyes.

'Oh no,' said Lucy quickly and definitely, convent education bringing roses to her cheeks, 'I hate photos of me.'

'That, my dear Lucy, is vanity,' said Jay. 'And why not? You're totally beautiful.'

'Vanity?' Lucy was intrigued.

'Yeah. Have you noticed, with group photos, everyone goes Bleeaggh!, I look terrible! You think you look better than any photo. And of course a photo never catches the way a face moves. I'd love to photo you. I'd have to take a few hundred and we might get one we both agree on. It is vanity. You have this picture of yourself — people fall in love with people who look like their idealised self, usually Narcissism. And in your case, why not? You're stunning,'

'I suppose. Well, you're not having my photo. I know what I'm giving you,' Lucy smiled on her secret.

'You give me poetry,' said Jay.

'Oh, shut up, Jay. It's too much.'

'Can anything be too much?' said Jay.

'I have to go,' said Lucy, as if scolding, eyes sparkling with pleasure, 'I'll see you when you're a year older.'

Eye to eye, they kissed — on the cheek — and parted.

CHAPTER EIGHT

Jay had a big thing about birthdays. Her parents had done birthday parties on a grand scale until she was about thirteen. Then stopped. Whether because they had ceased to be pleased about her birthday or simply because they were tired, she did not know. Her sixteenth birthday they had set the dining room table — her family usually ate in the kitchen — and her mother had imposed a reign of terror in her preparations. They had meant it to be special, but at the time, it had been dreadful, and when they began to sing Happy Birthday, Jay had burst into tears and run out of the room. Happy? The house was a terrifying tomb. And at sixteen she wished she had never been born.

Now, in *her* life she had relaxed and wonderful parties all year. But especially on her birthday. She got the food well out of the way mid-afternoon, devised a tongue-teasing cocktail, and asked all the people she loved. Thirty had been a party for fifty, and now had honed it down to a fabulous four. This year there was also Lucy.

She always worried that her friends wouldn't like one another. They usually did, but but but but . . . And especially she wanted Lucy to like her friends. She had asked Dionne the American ex-pat writer who never stopped talking, Jamie the drag queen who never stopped talking. Francis who stopped talking only sometimes, and Marina the theatre director who listened and had everyone else listening, a perfect example of it's not what you say, it's the way you say it.

Marina had that fabulous Gauloise and gin thee-ay-tah voice: which is why Jay had got to know her in the first place. And then Lucy.

She concentrated on cooking and wine, cleared all the piles of crap from the living room to the bedroom, agonised about a full spring clean, for what if Lucy stayed? Aw, hell, said the slut in her, it's me she's come to see not a tidy flat. I am what I am.

Dionne brought pink champagne and a new Nina Simone album. She darlinged Jay and kissed her mouth, all Chanel Crystalle and black silk shawls. She had come early, knowing the agony of being alone and waiting . . .

'So this could be The One, Jay, huh? But not yet?' she murmured, draped along the kitchen door.

'I think so. Hope so. Not for want of me trying. Shit!' Jay swore at saucepans, whirled eight things together. 'I have to change.'

'Don't worry, darling! If she doesn't know what a good thing you are, I feel sorry for her. But I shall give her the once over and deliver my inestimable verdict.'

Francis drifted in while Jay was changing.

'Sweetheart!' he said, hugging her silk-clad body, butterflying her just-rouged cheek. 'Best of luck! And happy birthday to you! Here's your prezzie. I feel like one of the three wise men, love, enjoy! It's Maui Waui, I got my surfer-ex to send me some. He wraps it in balls if you'll pardon the expression and puts it in M+M packets. Shall I make a joint? I've also brought you some of that queenie hooch you live on.'

'Good idea,' said Jay, kissing him. Jay's friends were very good on pink champagne. Suddenly she wondered if straight Lucy would mind the smoke? Ridiculous!

'You know this smouldering paragon of desire?' said Francis to Dionne.

'Not yet. I'm intrigued. Our Jay has been remarkably un-rampant for years!'

'Well, dear,' said Francis, 'This one's a real puzzle — no, I'll let you see for yourself.'

The bell rang. Shit!

But it was only the sensational Jamie, twirling a diamante choker on his index finger. Off-stage, no one would have looked at Jamie twice, standard rips in his faded jeans and political tee-shirt. The only thing he had in common with Cherry Morello, his stage persona, was a mega-mouth of repartee. The boy was born centre stage. He flung one leg round the door post, demanded a Las Vegas introduction and swanned into the room murmuring good evening, stopping when he saw Jay and looking totally bemused.

'I know your face . . .' he said, then bear-hugged her.

'Oh, pull —ease! I can't hug women. I'm a poof! Business is bad, love,' he said, plonking a flagon of cheap red on the table. 'Just a small token of my undying etceteras. Give me that smoke! *I* have arrived!'

'You kiss me before you get to reefer madness,' said Jay. 'Fasten it round my neck too, darling Jamie, thank you.'

'She's not here yet?' said Francis, raising an eyebrow. 'Should Jamie and I camp along to the pub and keep watch? It's awful to be last, isn't it?'

The doorbell rang.

Jay opened the door.

I Love Lucy.

Lucy in white silk Dynasty jacket, butterfly turquoise shirt, skin-tight velvet trousers, silver sandals. Kissed Jay on both cheeks.

'Happy Birthday,' she said; she smelt like spring flowers.

Francis and Jamie and Dionne said hi, Marina flew in

— exhausted, darling! — and Jay took a bucket of cocktails from the fridge.

'Darling!' said Francis. 'What is it?'

'You see,' said Jamie, leaning towards Lucy, 'Jay was a cocktail waitress in a previous incarnation — she has a Gift!'

'I thought she'd *had* a cocktail waitress, dear,' said Francis.

'Dyke's are very creative with exotic fruit,' said Jamie. 'An avocado in every orifice, so they say.'

'Or very ripe figs,' drawled Francis. 'I've seen Jay tongue out figs in the most suggestive manner, and positively drool over the sweet flesh of a mango. I can't imagine why.'

'I hope we're safe with this,' said Jamie, peering into the cocktail jug.

'Oh, she never recycles,' soothed Francis.

Thank God the rouge hid the blush, thought Jay, wishing she was a virgin for Lucy.

'And then there's vegetables,' said Jamie, 'A pound of very *firm* carrots please, Mr Greengrocer . . .'

'Oh, shut UP, you awful queens,' said Dionne. 'What is it, Jay?'

Jay poured cocktails for them all.

'Look Out For the Velvet Hammer,' she said, raising her glass.

'Happy Birthday, Jay,' they said, all her favourite friends and Lucy. Then —

'Wow!' said Lucy. 'I just felt the velvet hammer! Here!' She thumped her chest over the heartbeat.

Jay smiled, supremely confident. The first taste was fresh and innocuous, then it lit up the throat with a burst of sunshine: it hit the gut with a throb of heat. It had taken her days to invent this one.

'This is your present,' said Marina. She handed over a pink-tissued shape dripping with silver bows and gaudy ribbons. Marina always wrapped things so you didn't want to spoil them by opening. But inside was a crystal ball, a witch ball, old goldy glass with a fountain of trapped bubbles.

'It's a real crystal ball,' said Marina.

Jay loved everything about glass and felt the weight and smoothness. She kissed Marina.

'I'll tell your fortune later,' said Jamie. 'Gets better after a few drinks. You will meet a strange woman — that's safe, knowing the dives *you* frequent.'

'Happy birthday, Jay,' said Lucy. And gave her a square flat parcel.

'It's a baking tray, dear,' said Francis.

'Baking tray?' exploded Jamie. 'It's a cocaine mirror, oh give me some!'

'Shut up the pair of you,' said Jay, feeling like a kid at Christmas.

'I hope you haven't already got it,' said Lucy.

'It' was an LP of *Stabat Mater*, Pergolesi perfection, and a double of LP of mellifluous Pachelbel, Gluck, Bach et al.

'Thank you,' said Jay who adored all of them, 'I have the Pergolese, but it's totally worn out.'

Hardly surprising, since she'd played it non-stop since her Lucy dream, wept to it, soaked it in until it was her heartbeat, floated on the cloud of its beauty all through the Lucyless days. Her eyes met Lucy's and held them. God, she knew all right! No one can look back at you like that unless . . . She kissed Lucy and it didn't matter that somehow her lips landed only on her cheek. She put on the other record, save Pergolesi for later when surely they'd be alone. Oh yeah!

'The trouble is they've made most of them into cigar and wallpaper adverts,' said Lucy brightly. 'Or low-fat spreads.'

'Darling, I almost died!' said Francis. 'They've put

Satie over a building society commercial. Two hideous yuppies in tubular stainless steel sipping *minimalist* cocktails — no olives or fruit salad — God, give my ageing pectorals strength! — and contemplating how much they can borrow to house their sterile fucking, dear. I mean, they move into a mansion, they'll need both salaries for the next thousand years!'

'I know the one,' said Jamie. 'They'll get an au pair, some poor foreign bitch they can exploit.'

'That's hardly fair. I had an au pair once. She ran off with the silver. Literally,' said Lucy, sparkling into the conversation. Jay smiled. Marina took charge of Lucy, and she relaxed: Marina drawing people out was spectator sport.

And that was what Jay loved about her birthdays. Watching the people she loved most simply being together. She drifted from one conversation to another: Jamie and Francis in the Max Miller blue corner, Marina as audience, Dionne and Lucy in the Arts ring.

'Jay is a fabulous cook,' said Francis loudly at one point. 'Not that I'm dropping hints, darling!'

'Oh, she'll make someone a wonderful wife!' screeched Jamie.

And so late into the night. Finally the clock struck three, then four, finally Francis and Jamie lurched down the stairs arguing about how late the late night bars stayed open or had they got the energy to visit the Heath.

'I haven't got my Heath shoes on,' said Francis.

'Well it's quite dry, dear!'

'Oh I hope NOT!'

Marina seized a cab immediately, Dionne disappeared to the loo and Lucy stood to leave. Alone at last!

'Give us a kiss,' said Jay.

'Three,' said Lucy. 'Two continental and one on the lips.'

And her body went soft in Jay's arms. She almost parted her lips, then drew back.

'Darling!' breathed Jay, drawing her close, searching for her adorable lips again, 'stay with me. You know you want to.'

'I have to go home,' said Lucy.

'You will stay sometime? God, I want you so much! Oh, stay now!'

'Jay, you're drunk,' said Lucy, laughing and pushing her away, but gently. 'That was a lovely party. I like your friends. I'll see you on Monday.'

Jay followed Lucy as she put her coat on and went into the street.

'I love you, Lucy.'

Lucy wound down the window of her car and held her face up. Jay kissed her eyes, her brow, her chin . . .

'I've got to go.'

She went.

'Angel,' murmured Jay, waving to her along the dark road.

She raced upstairs again, paused at the door to touch her face and neck, everywhere Lucy had touched her.

'Well?' said Dionne.

'You tell me. Go on, tell me.'

Both Jay and Dionne had spent many a dawn listening to each other on the latest One and Only.

'Well,' said Dionne, extracting a half-bottle of brandy from her handbag. 'I take it it's too late to be sober or sleep? — Good. Then I'll begin.'

Dionne arranged herself along the couch. Jay poured brandy and sprawled on the floor. Earl Hines hit the turntable and Dionne spoke.

'One: Your Lucy is a stunner. Can you pick 'em, girl, or can you pick 'em! Two: she's fascinated. Eyes like saucers at those frightful queens we both know and love. Three: she likes you a lot.'

'Oh, I like it,' said Jay. 'Now for the bad news?'

'Well. Four: she's straight and a mummy. Had to be responsible all her life. Never had enough fun, thinks there's something endemically wrong with the pleasure principle. By which our kind live. Oh, I did my home-work, while you were screaming along with the boys! So, Jay, you've set yourself a wonderful conundrum. What a challenge! But don't be surprised if the answer's no. Have you really fallen head over etcetera, my dear? Of course you have. Does the Pope shit in the woods? I just worry, as usual, that I shall be mopping you up for months to come.'

'Maybe,' said Jay. 'I'm too far in to move back now. Don't care. Do care. God, isn't she wonderful!'

'What's your next move, you rambunctious dyke, you?'

'Oh, dinner, I think, chez moi,' said Jay lightly.

'Leap on her, Jay. Just leap and see what happens.'

A bird tweetered in the grey light through the blinds.

'Bed,' said Dionne, 'I'm staying with you, by the way, too broke for a cab. And I'm not too proud to be a surrogate. Make love to me, Jay.'

'You realise we did this on my last birthday? And then on yours?' said Jay as they snuggled close.

'What do you think drew me here?' said Dionne. 'I could get used to this bi-annual orgy, Jay dear. Shame we're not In Love, really. It could be very pleasant.'

CHAPTER NINE

Jay finished typing an article without any idea what she had typed.

Lucy, um, I wondered if you'd like to come over for dinner sometime, like tonight.

That was no good. Lucy would be busy.

I've got some amazing new music I'd like you to hear. You must come over soon.

And then she could say she'd like to borrow it. No.

Come over and I'll wine you and dine you and make love with you for the rest of your life.

So subtle!

'Have you got a minute, Jay?' Lucy had her serious office-work glasses on and a sheaf of papers.

I have a lifetime!

'Sure,' said Jay.

'Could you zip through this and see if it's OK? There's something wrong with it, and I just can't see it clearly.'

'Leave it to me.'

'Oh, you are *good.* Thank you.'

I'm actually very very evil, thought Jay with a wolfish grin. And sauntered down the corridor a half-hour later.

'Page three,' she said. 'Cut the second paragraph, it's confusing.'

'I'm very grateful,' said Lucy.

'Do you want to come over for dinner sometime?' said Jay, as if it had just occurred to her.

'Yes,' said Lucy, 'That would be nice. Let me get my diary.'

They booked a day, an evening.

And afterwards, Jay started her own diary, for her eyes only. It was all so unreal, she felt she had to write it down to prove it was happening, to have it and hold it to her heart.

Jay's Diary I

Forty-eight hours to seeing you. Not neurotic, that, just a way of parcelling out the time, and doing everything I need to. All accounted for and two and a half hours to spare. Time to think myself in and out of any last minute panic. Panics. But of course, not neurotic, no!

Off to the hairdresser. An hour.

Time on the bus to think: what do I wear? Launderette yesterday, everything's clean. Superstition, stop crossing your fingers. Last time I went to the hairdresser's I was so crippled with period pains I drank three instant g & t's on the bus. Not today. No gin for a month already. Have a drink at six-thirty. Not before. Brandy. You like brandy. Is there any hope of getting Greek brandy with its old gold seven stars? Should have thought of that before. Ho hum. Graffiti a heart, slash an arrow. I luv U. Have a cigarette. Another cigarette. Lousy crossword today, clever-clever, too many obvious anagrams. Shall I varnish my nails?

Gorgeous camp Sebastian goes to town, goes mad, keeps me laughing, lurid tongue, worldly-wise eyes: *you got a date then, darling?* Yeahhrrr I say. Hot stuff, Sebastian. *Well, dear, hope she's worth it!*

Read the stars in the magazines and the paper:
Today is your lucky day.
Grey is your lucky colour.
You are my lucky star.
And give it time! says Sebastian. *Don't wash it for three days! Give it time, I know you, you're so impatient.*

Yes, Sebastian, no Sebastian, my cup runneth over.

Now stop that. Shut up. Whatever happens will. No buts. Just get on.

Shop for food. Easy, do it in my sleep. *Do it.* Shut
the hell up. Time's moving on. Off-licence. Only one
bottle of pink left — omen?

JESUS! will you stop it? It's all bubbles. Oh, definite
omen, Greek brandy, Aegean witchcraft in its
classical bottle, lavishly labelled. I can do the Melina
Mercouri. Good good good.

Dress? Cook? Cook first. Messy cow, bloody garlic
all over clothes, not a good idea. Cooked. Clothes?

Old, new, borrowed, blue. Shoes, hair, shirt — oh,
yes, borrowed and grey — stonewashed jeans.
Casual, but good with this anarchic riot of hair.
Nearest you'll get to Tina Turner, dear! What a
woman!

Make-up. Seduction slap. Healthy outdoor look.
Easy on the kohl.

OK!

Sit with the music, blow a little smoke, time enough
to snap out of it, sip the brandy. She may not come.
Well, all *right*, you optimistic alter-ego, who rattled
your chain? Phone rings. She's not coming.

She is.

Bloody hell. Your voice . . . Thirty minutes. Open
the wine, lucky you've got a vacuum cork. Wrestling
with corks in front of her? Couldn't handle it.

Stick to brandy and Perrier. Hers the first sip of
pink champagne. Love her whatever. One of the best.
The best.

Pretzels and Mozart. Bayberry incense.

Now look here, you trembling ridiculous creature,
listen to me, nothing may happen and that has to be
OK too. Got it? Yizz. I got it.

But . . .

But but but but . . .

You're HOPELESS! (This from my pseudo-older-
and-wiser alter-ego).

Yizz Ah Know. Nice, ain't it?

Alter-ego sighs and looks wise.

So don't talk to me. Take the evening off.

Certainly! Exit offended alter-ego with money enough to go to the pictures.

Alone at last! Time to reflect, gather myself together, brush my teeth again, roll a . . .

Shit! You're at the door.

How come every time I see you you're even lovelier than I remember. You're breathtaking, sparkling, your lovely hair is swept up to a glossy oriflamme, you're a study in black and white, your merry eyes are *wonderful.*

Talk slow. That way I don't appear as nervous as my skippety-hop heart. Good God, I've known you long enough and why the hell have my knees decided to take their annual vacation at this precise moment?

Music. You say Fats Waller. Sit. Come back, knees, all is forgiven. Melina Mercouri just as marvellous as I thought. Glad for the glasses, love lustre.

Your eyes.

Mouth on careless automatic. *Oh, God, your eyes.*

Pretzels, I say, for God's sake, bring on the pretzels.

More jazz — more jazz. Tapes crash all over my desk. Hysteria. Inanimate objects reflect my mood. Hopeless to try and impress *you* with my slender collection of classical music. Stick to jazz, home ground.

More Melina Mercouri, hi, knees, glad you could make it, check food, what the hell that's never a problem.

Are we going to eat pretzels or are we going to eat?

Oh, yeah, food, yeah. More Melina Mercouri.

Can't eat much anyway, your eyes, being, presence, hands, mouth, hair, *You* marvellous *woman*, you.

Satie, God, if I could write like Satie writes music!

If I could just reach out and touch your
face . . .

I love you.

Enter alter-ego. Lousy film and what the hell is
going on here? Just piss off to a nightclub, dear, come
back in the wee small hours. GO!

More froth. Perrier too, esses beginning to go.

When I fell in love with you, I say, feeling lyrical . . .

I don't think you are in love with me, you cut in,
fixing me with your eyes.

My heart double flips. Something in the air. Written
you four stories, showed you one. Show you two. You
show me an article you've written. It's brilliant, clear,
cool, precise and humorous . . .

I want to touch you.

No, you say, all in control, we are not going to sleep
together.

Honey, who said a word about sleeping?

I push you like hell. Maybe I can take, sometime I
can take, but I can't take no from you. Yet I am
amazed when we do kiss. Your lips are so soft, your
hair is silky, your body is warm and so tender.

Oh, I don't want to stop. Pushing my luck is my
favourite occupation. With you. Love your cheeks,
your chin, your ears, your brow, your neck, I love
your perfectly beautiful breasts, like holy wine.

And then just when we might not *stop*, oh my love,
my virgin forest and me your virgin explorer, it is
time, just like that, to stop. We're worth so much
more. I don't want to make hasty and furtive love
with you. Got to do this with our eyes wide open.

You sit beside me in my arms. Jesus! You are
lovelier than I dreamed. You say you feel safe with
me. You are. I feel sanctified. You say you've never
kissed a woman like that before. Of course, I realise,
dazed, of course you haven't. How strange! And I

have never kissed a woman like you before, I've never kissed you before.

Would you do something for me?

Anything, sure, of course, what? I know you're going, my heart fears the worst . . . I keep perfectly still.

Would you kiss my breasts again? It felt so . . .

Something for you? Something so indescribably ecstatic for me. You go to undo your shirt, your silk shirt alive with the warmth of your breasts . . . I wouldn't dream of allowing it, it's my pleasure, I do it. And you undo your bra, never kissed a woman who wears a bra before.

God, I love you.

You give me your breasts and hold me close. You are warm in my arms, your body right next to mine. If my lips had words for the wondrous feeling of your breasts and nipples I'd say them. But there are no words good enough for perfection. And I could die and go to heaven when I hear you making wordless muted sounds beside me and feel your lips kiss my brow so gently.

I love you so.

CHAPTER TEN

Jay's Diary II

I knew L. would take a holiday sometime. What I didn't realise was that her holiday started the day after she'd had dinner with me, she was going to Italy to look at churches with her beloved son. For fourteen days. I made myself pretty busy: got pissed, went and screamed at Jamie, saw a million movies, realised with horror that that ate up only a week.

A repeat performance the next week punctuated by a postcard from L. showing the entire Sistine Chapel ceiling on the front, and missing the word LOVE on the back. Ho hum. Three days before she came back, I cleaned the flat, bought a new jacket and five bright new cotton shirts, stayed sober, worked like hell on the magazine in a way that made Francis 'gasp and stretch his eyes'.

'All this and you haven't even got under the duvet with her yet, dear! God help us when you do!'

But I have clammed up about L. Feel superstitious. Maybe if I keep mum and keep my fingers crossed — what did my father always say when I couldn't have something: 'Them that ask don't get, them that don't ask, don't want.' He thought it was funny and who *needs* a Mary Poppins LP, a Beatles poster, a sequinned belt, anyway. Well, I did and didn't get and now I have all these things.

She's back tomorrow. Could this be why I'm ironing with a face-pack on?

To Aldgate then I came, burning, burning after a Badedas bath, when things happen!

Flowers at her door, good God, it's less than nine in the morning . . . but she, of course, is already here.

Standing at her office door, fool with hearts and flowers. She has positioned herself behind her desk, and will not meet my eyes.

'Hi,' I say, 'welcome back.'

'Are these for me?' she says, with (feigned?) surprise, 'That's kind.'

'You have a nice holiday' *Or some such bullshit.*

'Oh lovely.' *Let's keep it civilised.*

'Coffee?' *I want to kiss you.'*

'That would be nice.' *Maybe we don't have to talk about it.*

I make coffee, she phones around, shifts papers, I can't say a word I mean. Think I must be blushing, and maybe she is too or is it her English rose complexion kissed, fuck, there I go, kissed (I should be so lucky!) by sudden Mediterranean sunshine? We drink coffee. I recall that there is a meeting this afternoon to discuss the paper we wrote. I'm being allowed onto her ecologically correct territory, and no one there will know how we kissed and almost, as good as, made love . . . but I will and she will.

'Look, Jay,' she says, all bright and brisk, like there was a fascinating bird on the windowsill she just *had* to show me, 'we've got to cool it.'

'Cool it?' I say, feeling ice cubes drop slowly into this volcano of longing. Should I have grabbed her this morning? Who knows? Not me . . .

'Yes,' she says, rushing through her script, 'we have plans to work together. It's not a good idea.'

File this love under N.B.G. I am mute, catatonic. Feel the tears, nod, my ironed clothes crumple to rags. And we have a meeting at six.

'See you,' I say and escape to City Road, where an off-licencee is opening and looks up surprised to see an office yuppie (his definition) among the line of winoes so early in the morning-o! Theirs is cider and Carslberg special and Emva Cream, and mine is a bottle of brandless brandy and lo-cal ginger ale, ever figure conscious as if anyone gave a damn.

Francis takes in the scene at ten. I am half-pissed and brilliant, Francis takes me for egg and chips and strong tea and tells me to give it up. I should be so lucky to be able to.

But L. knows nothing of this. By five I am sober and handle the meeting with a superb

professionalism borrowed from Mildred Pierce and
Mommie Dearest. She hasn't a clue and asks me out
for a drink. We chat, and I mentally award myself
thirteen Oscars.

She relaxes. What was she expecting — Baby Jane?
She feels she has to say something.

'I was very drunk, Jay,' she says in a rush, 'I didn't
mean that to happen.'

Drunk?

'I know you were. I was too. But I mean it, you
know.'

'You'll just have to give me time,' she says. 'I'm a
very slow sort of person usually.'

Lights the embers of my fool heart with this
maybe. If all she needs is time to say *yes, I'll be your
lover*, then she has all the time in the world. I've
waited long enough for love, for her. Does she mean
days weeks months years? Not the time to ask.

'I won't stop asking you,' I say, and she looks
guarded, pleased, looks like she's trying not to show
anything.

Home alone to the immaculate discipline of writing
sonnets. (Ha!) Feel like Pam Ayres, the rhymes are no
problem, but it all comes out doggerel.

But my In Love body forgets about food and sleep
and produces its own adrenalin to keep me flying
through every hour. Francis is knocked out and so
am I. I seem to be doing more and more advisory art
stuff for Lucy's magazine, positively volunteering, my
dear, what is happening?

What's happening is that I have a reason for rising,
for living, for laughing. Two glasses of wine send me
high over the rainbowed moon. And then there are
the dreams, more vivid than the live-long day.

CHAPTER ELEVEN

Jay's Diary III

So suppose you turn to me and say *yes*.

The Yes that launches a thousand sky-rockets just as my heart is a catherine-wheel the second I fall in love with you. And has been ever since.

Yes means a time for us to be together, us and only us in a place that is beautiful and special and quiet and doesn't know just how amazing a love is about to transform it into one of those Indian summer memories that make deaf old ladies grin knowingly, when you think they are dead in a deckchair on the sea front. But they are not dead, just dreaming, and you have no idea how passionately their stiff and shaking limbs once burned.

The place is off the beaten track, two bumpy miles wrecking the car suspension and who gives a damn? Not you, my dear, with your frankly fabulous soul, and not me, alive alive-o! There is nobody else on this earth who even knows we are here.

We are both appalling about food. You forget to eat, and you think it doesn't matter, and I can't eat when you're around. But we are trying to be sensible. So we go through the motions of feeding ourselves.

One thing about *us*, before love and ever since — B.L. and A.L. — is we never run out of things to say. Funny how tongue-tied I feel right now, over the table from you, my love, I feel safest pouring wine.

We both shake when we're nervous. And go cold.

But my arms round you, your arms holding me, and the shivering stops and welds us still and close and still closer.

B.L. I had these passionate blouse-ripping fantasies, the sort where you dissolve on a bearskin rug and explode with ecstasy.

A.L. I am learning a reality of slow warmth. Slow and sure.

Like there is now, holding each other in the middle of nowhere.

We shall have music wherever we go.

And now in the firelight there is only the best of music to play.

Notes that arabesque around the magnificent abundance of trees in the wind, shaking sea-grey, spring-green, ashen-blue.

I am lying in the grass dazed by the sun and the busy ants, by the myriad humming galore of a river on a summer afternoon. A dragonfly skims a path through the tips of the rushes.

We are on a shore of white sand too hot to stand still for a moment, great breakers surf and trip to swathes of foam as we dart into the solid black and lovely shade.

The rose garden at dawn. I watch you free-wheeling along a vine-wrapped colonnade, and pause under an archway wrought in stone and lovely with purple flowers ringing in the new light.

On this high hill, the wind whips your face chill; the wind drops and your cheeks are burning; you can see the patchwork of seven counties sweeping and dissolving to misty far green at your feet, rising again to heather-blue mountains melting to pure white cloud.

Oh, the dawn when shadows skeeter ahead of the sure fluid sunlight, back to their night.

We are held, stunned surely under a crescent moon, thrilled by ice-white stars and the scent of magnolia, your dress a sweep of silver through a baroque balcony entwined with dusk-white roses . . .

Look at you now — you take my breath. I look at you now, with the flame gold lilting on the fine planes of your face and caressing your fine fingers. In the glow the lazy blue smoke of a cigarette folds in slow waves to vanish in the sepia shadows of the room Everything about *us* says *come here, you*, and our fingertips are first to arc between us and hover on cheeks, lips, chin. We are swimmers in slow motion, we glide together through clear and wordless waves, strokes of pure genius.

Mid afternoon gives us a moment when the heart of light in a leaf trembles russet rainbows.

Dawn brings a gift of spider webs flashing diamonds on sea-grey gorse.

Midday burns the sky azure, bleaches to blind dazzle a field of ripe wheat.

Midnight and a silvered road of dreams, a black field shot with a million bursts of white — the name is glow-worm, the sight is magic.

Spring leaves of pure sap green silver-haired as a child's arm.

I am in love with *you*, the feeling drives me, drives me crazy, tumbles me in a drum.

To reach *you*, to touch *you*.

CHAPTER TWELVE

That spring was magic. A rare sneak preview of

summer in the city, ice-cream regency houses linked
with solid tree silhouettes against a sky as blue as blue.
Trees in the park misted over with young green, bright
spring yellow flowers crowding front gardens; embassy
lawns starred with daisies; snowdrop beds, municipal
grass studded with crocuses. Jay drove as if inspired,
drinking it all in. She made fresh tapes to play in the car,
and grinned at the luxury of traffic jams in the
company of Louis Prima and Sidney Bechet. She drove
as if Lucy was beside her — usually she cursed every
cut-throat city driver — and sucked the hell out of a
row of pre-rolled cigarettes, cigarettes rolled hastily at
red lights, slamming in and out of gear. These days of
wonder, she felt graciously pleased with her life;
keeping her self-promise not to be heavy with Lucy,
thinking herself under the skin and into the mind of the
woman she loved.

It must be strange to be the object of my affection,
she thought idly, especially if all you've had is hard-
chested men doing their best but never sure. Because
when Jay had first kissed a woman, she knew she had
come home, it was what she was born for.

Extravagant long evenings, she consulted her good
fairies.

Dionne said: 'Well, if she's had a necking session or
two with you, you wicked dyke, she's obviously
interested.'

Francis said: 'I couldn't have your patience, darling!
Could your Lucy be playing a little game — sorry! I take
that back. I am merely a dyke-hag. *Stunned* at the
privilege, but I shall never understand you. Good luck!'

Marina said: 'It's very strange, Jay. I've known you In
Love, but never quite like this. I worry that you'll get
hurt. You always get hurt.'

Jamie said: 'Christ, dear! I'm celibate, don't ask *me!*
I've probably got AIDS anyway, and I'm hopelessly

jealous. The doctors will tell me if I get ill. I should have been a lesbian! Don't see how you can stand the celibacy when you don't have to. There'll be a fucking explosion one of these days when you do finally **Do It**. And weren't you the dyke who was extolling the virtues of the single life only months ago? Yes! You were!'

Jay said: 'I don't know what I'm doing, it's never been this way before, can't go on anything else, but this time I'm not going to fuck up.'

Hm, said her friends, and hmmmm said Jay herself to her self when she was alone.

And she had devised a hook for time with Lucy. What a fucking chameleon I am, she mocked herself. The hook was an exhibition they could work on together, a definitive work on pollution and the arts, the environment and how artists respond to it. Lucy had been approached by an international humanist organisation, there was funding, and Lucy was raring to go. But needed some kind of help: she'd spoken about it for months before and was utterly thrilled when Jay drawled an interest. Jay sketched it out as a glass bead game lavishly illustrated; the square squalor of modern conurbations as a desperate attempt to assert human life, defying destruction and repelling nature after wars and disasters. The way 'civilisations' had to make their mark, just in case they might disappear without trace.

Lucy bit. Jay realised she was flattered at being asked, realised that Lucy thought of her as somehow daringly on the wrong and the right side of the track all at the same time. And the exhibition *would* be important, she told herself, when a flow of desire swept her away at the thought of being with Lucy, time allotted to their togetherness.

'You've got it bad,' said Francis.

'It'll keep me out of the pub, dear,' said Jay. 'I reckon the way to this woman's heart is through her mind.'

'Heart? Mind?' said Francis with a giggle. 'Pardon me being basic, but is it going to be nights over a hot typewriter with champagne and a little heavy breathing on the side?'

'We live in hope,' said Jay.

The first exhibition meeting was at Lucy's flat. Where they roughed out the areas they could cover, and possible sources of material. Lucy wanted a pamphlet by way of introduction; Jay said, let's just get all the information together. Lucy had borrowed the office word-processor. The hours burned by on the green screen, and when they finally flopped in Lucy's living room, sipping brandy, a key turned in the lock and in came the charmingly dishevelled one and only son. Like he owned the place. Jay withdrew a little.

'Jem!' said Lucy, switching into mum mode, 'have you eaten? This is Jay — oh, you met before.'

St Patrick's Day. Ho hum.

Jeremy smiled with Lucy's elfin charm, stretched, yawned and said:

'Don't fuss, mum. Hi, Jay. I was shattered when I met you last. I gather you're a leading light in the arts — these are mine for my sins.'

He indicated the pictures lining the walls. He knew he was good, and Lucy was blushing slightly. Maternal pride? Or was she confounded by two separate parts of her life coming together?

'I like that one,' said Jay, pointing to a pagan woodland scene. 'But I'm no judge, Jeremy, just a hack.'

'Don't work mum too hard!' he said, glancing at his watch.

He poured a glass of wine and appeared settled.

'Did you call back the Cartieri Gallery?' said Lucy suddenly.

'No,' he said, in a long-suffering tone.

'Well, you must, Jem, they've left three messages.'

He loafed to his feet, and put his hands on Lucy's shoulders.

'Worry, worry, worry. I'll call them tomorrow, mum. I'd better sleep. Nice to meet you, Jay.'

He loped upstairs. The atmosphere had held a certain smoky glow, he had fragmented it. So sure of himself, so sure of Lucy.

'What's he doing these days?' asked Jay. Not that she gave a damn, but Lucy's mind was obviously on him.

'Portraits,' said Lucy briefly. 'He wants to do mine.'

'I'll buy it,' said Jay.

'Oh, he'll make me look a hundred and three,' said Lucy. 'All these lines!'

'I love your lines,' said Jay. 'They're a map of who you are. You can tell what a person's like from their lines — you make your face.'

'Yes?'

'Well, you've done a lot of laughing. And worrying. And crying. But, by God, lady, you've decided to survive.'

'Which line's that?' said Lucy grinning. It was so easy to flatter her, she took it like a sixteen year old who's never heard it before.

'Oh, that's the chin,' said Jay, 'that chin says *don't fuck with me, fella!*

Lucy smiled.

'Time to go home,' she said, and kissed Jay gently on the cheek at the door. Jay held her hand and brushed her adorable fingers with her lips.

'I think this exhibition's really going to happen. I knew I couldn't do it alone,' Lucy said.

Driving home, she wondered. Jem still lived at home — was that why Lucy had no lovers? Their next meeting was a month ahead. And that was at Jay's place.

CHAPTER THIRTEEN

Jay's first task concerned nature forms and architecture, the adaptation of natural societies versus the hard-edged impersonality of modern cities. One of Jay's favourite themes. Nothing but the best for Lucy, and that meant a month of sober evenings honing every flip phrase so that it made a point. Jay was given to grandiloquent rambling, and had to check herself. She spent hours with magazine archives for illustrations, even spent an afternoon in the Royal Horticultural Society library. A deliciously dotty old lady afternoon: the three other researchers there had at least two hundred and fifty years of living between them. Jay had taken her camera to photo the leather-bound treasures of the seventeenth century, where even the language was rounded in sepia sworls, respectful of rhythm, season, nature and wholeness.

After three weeks, even she was satisfied. Not a comma out of place. Oh, good child, she teased herself, if only you'd done this at school and art college, you'd have got a first. But she had only ever pulled the stops out for people she loved and respected. One or two teachers and tutors had inspired her. But no one had ever moved her like Lucy. Oh, would she be pleased! Hell, if she wasn't, at least Jay was. A rare feeling.

So she hoovered the floor, made a leisurely and politically correct lasagne, whipped egg whites, chilled good wine, luxuriated in the lion-gold tobacco Dionne had brought her from France, wondered about writing to the manufacturers about distribution in England.

Only then did she let herself watch the clock to the strains of Beethoven's *Apassionata*. Oh, to live abroad! But whenever she'd been free to emigrate, she'd fallen in love and put it out of the question. In fact, the day before the I Love Lucy St Patrick's Day, she'd been told of a good job with the British Council in the Gilbert Islands. But why go half-way round the world to find Lady Happiness when She works next door to you? Jay stacked her manuscript and photos, sat with a cigarette and a glass of Pouilly Fumé, only Lucy needed to complete her freesia-scented scene.

Lucy arrived, drained and tight-lippèd, Jeremy had been having trouble with his girlfriend, and Lucy had provided the two a.m. shoulder all week.

'Good old mum,' she said, sighing. 'It must be the artistic temperament. His father was — similar.'

Jay rubbed her screaming shoulders.

'Have a drink,' she said.

Lucy threw down three glasses in succession like water in the broiling sun. Jay played Satie and waited for when Lucy would stop shaking. She held Lucy's hand still to light her cigarette.

'I shouldn't have come,' said Lucy swiftly. 'I haven't done my bit.'

'Well, let's just eat and relax,' said Jay. But while she was setting out plates, a tongue of fury ripped along her spine. So golden boy had flipped — this week? Lucy had had three weeks before then, and *still* done nothing? She tried to think into motherhood, though Jeremy was twenty-five.

'Did you expect this to happen?' she said, as Lucy took small hard bites. She might as well have been eating spam.

'No,' said Lucy, 'it all blew up last weekend. I thought they were getting on fine.'

We had a month, thought Jay, I've worked my ass off

for this exhibition and you've done nothing. Patience, mon vieux, she told herself, the lady's had a hard time. But when she took Lucy's hand and smiled at her, trying to convey some of the warmth she felt, Lucy's lips smiled for a half-second and she took her hand away.

Jay's spine spat flame-tipped arrows.

'Show me what *you've* done,' said Lucy.

Jay shrugged and shoved the pages and photos towards her.

'Listen, we could get going on your bit now,' she said.

'No,' said Lucy. 'Couldn't.'

Jay wished for telepathy. To her mind, Lucy looked like she could do with a huge warm hug. But had rejected her hand. Was sitting, one knee over her other leg, body language *don't touch me.* Jay sprawled on the floor, sipped wine, stopped herself grabbing Lucy's grabbable ankles, held herself back. What to do.

'How have you been otherwise?' she said.

'Oh, busy,' said Lucy. End of subject.

'Is Jeremy still working?'

'Yes. Like a fiend. He said to tell you he'd like to paint you. This will amuse you, he said he liked older women.'

'That gives us something in common,' said Jay.

Lucy ignored this. And all too soon the stilted conversation ran out. Jay fell silent, slapped child who doesn't know why.

'It's OK,' said Lucy. 'It's just one of those things. It's OK.'

You won't touch me, you haven't done a thing for this goddam exhibition you were so all fired up about, and it's OK?

Jay became slashingly dykey, rolling one cigarette after another, was unashamedly heterosexist, never raised her voice above a steely drawl, though her throat was screaming with all the things she couldn't say, her body bruised with the feeling of being trivialised. Why the hell had Lucy come over? What did she want? Did she want to be seduced? Did she want to be loved? She looked so unhappy, Jay didn't know what to do.

She knelt in front of Lucy, clasped her hands.

'Lucy, you're with me. It's OK. I love you.'

'I know you do. And I must go.'

Just that and she was gone.

Jay hurled the empty plates at the wall, turned up Millie Jackson on the stereo and stamped back when her neighbours hammered on the ceiling.

CHAPTER FOURTEEN

Jay borrowed Lucy's pre-occupied indifference for the next little while. As Lucy chatted (work, son) over coffee, a red cloud, just like in the movies and purple fiction, blocked out her sight. Weeks passed. By now, they should have had an outline to present to the sponsors. Which Lucy knew, so why should Jay remind her.

'Darling,' said Francis, 'or should I say Ms. Razor-blades, could we attempt lunch?'

'Sure,' said Jay. 'Only a certain topic is censored, a certain party's name is not to be mentioned.'

'Alleluia!' said Francis, and sparkled like a tinsel waterfall, got Jay laughing and wondering recklessly why she'd ever bothered with the bloody woman. Always she neglected her friends when she was In Love, and regretted it afterwards. But so did they: friends were for fun and solace. Friends were for life.

She spent many evenings watching Jamie, whose scathingly political drag show was wowing the entire circuit. She became taxi driver, purveyor of fine wines, lender of lurex and drag-hag extraordinaire. Alone, she was given to melodramatic sonnet sequences and masturbation. She felt like a fool.

Finally, one evening, fighting with the dented lock to her car, she was surprised by Lucy's voice.

'Jay,' she said, with what sounded like pleasure, 'I haven't seen you for ages. What about this exhibition?'

'Well, *what* about this world-wide exhibition?' said Jay staring Lucy between the eyes.

Lucy flushed.

'How angry are you with me?' she said. The right/wrong question.

Shit! Them there eyes! Jay's heart did a Pavlov tattoo.

'I'm angry,' she drawled. 'Don't fuck with me, lady.'

'I deserved that,' said Lucy. 'I'm sorry. Let's meet.'

'Yeah?' said Jay, like who-gives-a-shit.

'Yes,' said Lucy. 'I *am* sorry. I'll come over to you.'

As if it was penance. They co-ordinated diaries and Jay congratulated herself on refusing to smile.

So Lucy came over. Jay had done wine, and decided, fuck it, there's always a take-away if the bitch is hungry. She did dope all afternoon, spaced out to Nina Simone and Marvin Gaye — why was there no one better to wank to than Marvin Gaye? — and decided:

OK, LADY, IF WE'RE WORKING, LET'S WORK!

The bell rang. Either Lucy was feeling chastened or doing a damn good act that way. She had her introduction for the exhibition and Jay read it like she didn't know who'd written it. It was good, but sparse, abrupt even — like Lucy? Her lips tightened.

'I have this critical streak,' she said.

'Yes?' said Lucy.

'If you can stand it,' said Jay and chose her words. 'It's an impersonal thing. You have the substance here but it's too economic. I don't think there's any need to talk down to people, but you can't assume specialist knowledge.'

Lucy looked like a bright little girl, and Jay snapped into the role of brisk helper. She took the bones of Lucy's text, then fleshed them out a little here and there. Flesh. At one point, Lucy's hand brushed hers, and she managed to ignore it.

At ten, she made omelettes. The perfect hostess, on her guard. And then it was midnight. Lucy relaxed in an easy chair. Jay poured brandy.

'So that's all done,' murmured Lucy. 'You're very good. I'm sorry about last time. I get scared.'

She leaned forward and held Jay's hand. Jay melted, knelt upright and kissed her neck.

'What's killed me,' she breathed, 'is not being able to touch you.'

'I've been touching you with my eyes,' said Lucy. 'Only you wouldn't look at me.'

Jay flayed herself for what now appeared gross and hasty: her need for real contact, skin to skin. Because now she was touching Lucy and time stood still.

'I couldn't look at you,' she said, Lucy's fine hands on her shoulders. 'I was so angry. I felt trivialised.'

'Never feel that,' said Lucy, 'Oh, God, I feel like I'm sixteen again. Do you know what I've missed?'

Her hands moved over Jay's shoulders.

'I remember holding your breasts,' said Lucy. 'Last time . . .'

we stand in the hall, your fabulous eyes searched mine – read my eyes, one last and wonderful caress, shy love, love

you are gone into the early morning dark
night-rainbows dazzle everywhere you have been

'For God's sake get under my shirt,' said Jay low and urgent, stunned as their lips met, Lucy's tongue shyly exploring her mouth. She ripped her shirt from her jeans and her hands held Lucy's head like fine porcelain. She eased her shaking hands against the smooth perfection of Lucy's breasts, thumb drawing those soft warm nipples hard and hot.

'But I have to get back,' said Lucy. 'Jem needs me now.'

JEM needs you now? Jem needs you NOW? This boy of yours is twenty-five years old, old enough to father children and break hearts. And just selfish enough to demand that momma bird flies back to the bloody nest – surely to God not tonight, you can't do this to me, Lucy, I'm going to crack with all this nothing. Jay took a deep breath and nuzzled Lucy's neck.

'You think I don't?'

'I feel safe with you. Give it time,' said Lucy. 'It's all so strange. Don't know what's happening. Give me time.'

'Lucy,' said Jay, 'you have all my time.'

'Thank you,' said Lucy softly, hugged her again and went off into the night.

The blessed night, even alone, brought Jay an awareness of her body, as if she were phosphorescent with stars and meteorites. For the first time in all these barren weeks, she wrote poem after poem, cursed that Interflora wasn't a 24-hour service and swore never to doubt again.

I love Lucy, she breathed on her eighth orgasm and slept like a loved and wanted baby.

CHAPTER FIFTEEN

Jay resolved to be a little more eclectic in her renewed passion. This time, no mistakes. She and Lucy would get out of this one alive, and all in one piece. She spent time with her friends and restricted herself to ten minutes on the perfection of Lucy. Unless she was drunk, when her mouth curled around the delicious pleasure of The Beloved. But she hung on to herself.

And since her birthday, she had been seeing more of Dionne than she had for years. It wasn't In Love, they knew each other too well to risk that. But when they met, dinner at home, dinner out, dinner at Dionne's, they had taken to sleeping together, sometimes just that, warmth in Dionne's huge silky bed or hers, and sometimes a deep and wonderful sexual fusion, neither planned nor yearned after. Dionne was between tough young lovers.

'This won't do,' she said to Jay suddenly. 'This is turning into an *affaire*, darling, and I don't want to. We're both very bad at it and I'm damned if I'm losing my best friend.'

'I thought it was OK,' said Jay. 'Two old dykes having a little long overdue fun?'

'Jay, honey, no. I've started thinking about you between times. I'm kinda intense, my dear, and I don't want to do that to you. And I've suddenly started to resent those starry eyes of yours and your Lucy. Not seriously, but I know me. Come on, sweetie, what if I started getting it on with one of my baby dykes, what would you feel? We're making a habit of this lovely sex thing, and we're both the type to want more. Pretty damn soon too if we're not careful. Hey?'

'I guess,' said Jay bleakly.

Yeah, she'd started to need Dionne, pushed it aside since they were friends, and between friends you could take it for granted, since it was. But surely, she reasoned, where there could be no reason, surely sex doesn't have to bring with it the pain of need, longing, the fear of rejection? Sex for fun? Surely . . .?

But just as surely, she knew Dionne was right.

'I love touching you,' she said, clinging for a moment.

'Loon, we've always touched. I love fucking with you. Best lover I've ever had and so on. But this isn't — hell, it isn't in love. And you know it. Against the odds, that's what I want. I want to be In Love. And it isn't you.'

And so farewell to that pocket of warmth, thought Jay. It made sense and she didn't like it. While nothing had been expressed it was fine, but words bloody words and a self-conscious constraint was thrust upon them.

OK, suppose she was In Love with Dionne. Just suppose. All the movement theorists said you could love more than one person, and had strings of wrecked relationships to prove it. Jay had never known it to work for more than weeks. Then jealousy and anxiety moved in and squatted like diseased vagrants. Conditioning? If it was conditioning it was deep as her bones and marrow.

So what was love? Licence to kill? A crime of passion? Licence to allow another person to dictate the rising of the sun, the seasons of the moon?

Home, alone, Jay played through the last time Dionne had come over. The last time they'd made love, or would, probably. What would it be like to be In Love with Dionne rather than just loving her? She wrote in her diary, that long-abandoned Chinese embroidered silk book: her unfinished testimony to Lucy.

To Lucy? To Dionne? To Love itself.

CHAPTER SIXTEEN

You come into my room. Oh, pretty woman, *walk* my way! More than pretty. Glossy surfers' hair, eyes blue as a robin's egg and a dreamy far-off ocean at dawn. The kind of nose that flirts with the idea of being stroked and kissed and nibbled. Lips holding the promise of an aw-shucks smile, and flirting with every syllable. A chin I could write a prelude about firm and fine over the symphony of your neck.

And tho' I know the smooth curve of your naked shoulders, right now, and now it's right, you are wearing a moth-mauve shirt and a chic built-up soap-opera heroine jacket. Memory ignites a garland of fairy lights around the shifting folds of fabric, teases me knowing your nipples' strawberry centre, the soft heat of your naked breasts.

You delight my eyes; your voice delights my ears; your being here thrills me. It's a Saturday night, the night that's all right for late and mega-high for Sunday is a day of rest and you've chosen to spend this Saturday night — let me not presume! — evening, with me. And a whole lot more besides . . .

We drink brandy filled with lazy sunshine. You talk to me. I listen and like. Very much. You are the only woman I know — apart from Lucy — who wears skirts and dresses and make-up and turns me on more powerful than a monsoon with all the steam and heat . . . And tonight, oh my elegant darling, your skirt is a rainbow of shimmering gold and mauve and tan and cerise. Lying across your knees like a maharani's scarf.

I conjure an Ethiopian slave to fan you with peacock feathers.

Of course you wear black — stockings? I hope so! — or maybe tights. Who gives a damn, certainly not me, caressing your lovely legs with my eyes. Which you probably know. Probably like. A lot. I concentrate on your face and say something back to you. But when you talk I stray back to your ankles in a fantasy of exploring there with my tongue. Your feet are a mystery in shoes that look like velvet, look like suede, fit you and enhance you and tantalise my warm mouth with desire every time you move your toes.

Your hands are playing with the glass I gave you. Sparkle fine and curving like I remember your breasts in my hands. Well, it *would* be kinda fun to suck your fingers and take me a mouth-walk on the planet of your palms . . .

When I offer you champagne you laugh in a way that only you have, like a stream all at once a delighted cascade into this deep swirling pool of warm humour.

'You are *naughty*!' you say, spacing your words with a gleam in your wise-sky eyes, 'OK. Let's drink a bottle of champagne . . .'

Well, I kinda knew you'd say that, but had forgotten the unique thrill of the way only you can say things.

I don't know why we drink so much and come up smelling of roses. I don't know why we drink so much. I don't know why we drink. I don't know why we . . . the hell I don't!

And you are laughing again, shaking your head, it's what's-happening-I-don't-believe-this-honey time again.

What amazes me, apart from the instant MGM jungle scenery that leaps out of the walls the minute you walk in, the way the carpet has become an over the rainbow poppy field, only it's rose petals, what amazes me is we don't run out of things to say.

Well I guess we have a lot to catch up on, like the whole of our lives seeing as we finally got to say hello to each other only years ago. I have this urge to show you my childhood stamp collection, just that I don't have one.

Time lilts by on the jazz schmaltz I adore, memories, blues and brandy. You start off being coy about drinking brandy. What the hell did I get it for — to have it sit on the fucking shelf? Much rather see you drink. And much much much much rather feed you brandy with my mouth which hasn't done so much smiling since I was knee-high to a grasshopper and didn't know just how much fun this life could be.

BUT
Let us not forget
Let us not
Oh, let's . . .?
I feel totally new world extravagant around you.

You are drunk and so am I and in bed you turn your back to sleep. Do you really imagine that your back is less inspiring than your front? I'd happily joyously ecstatically fuck your eyebrows, darlin'. As it happens. And I can't and won't hold back when you grind your sensational ass against me, a woman is only human. You tell me to seduce you when you're sober, sweetheart, I'll take a chance on now. I want to kiss you like a butterfly on mescaline, all over in a flurry of delirium, I want to bite you to the bones, to be so close to you there materialises a planet called us.

I adore fucking you. Feel it's what I was born for. Everything in me shoots high like a hot spring, like the fourth of July when my fingers meet your flowing cunt, my face twisted in an agony of pleasure. Inside you I feel dizzy like a tango, the rose of your breast between my teeth. Inside you, inside you, I can never get enough of being inside you, makes me break apart, clench my teeth, drag breath so deep my head spins.

It's nothing to do with coming, it's everything to do with intoxication, flesh-frenzy, reckless rampant effervescent fever. Coming is easy, roundabouts and swings, and fucking you is a big dipper with no brakes flying out across a midnight ocean under a chandelier of stars.

You say it's not OK just to take, darling, angel, siren, demon, goddess, fucking you fucking canonises me. And then you plunge into me, my spine shatters and floats in hyperspace, and I know — don't know what it is, but it is.

I like, too, like very much, like a drowning person *likes* the feel of solid ground on their delirious tide-washed body. I LIKE that you tell me about it, your flesh impatient with words, you say: go inside me — yeah — yeah — no — more — and your body whiplashes head to toe, the ill-appreciated G spot, baby you got it.

In the morning you smoke. I smoke.

We have to talk, you say.

I just knew this had to be coming. I groan and hide my head in your side. Sure we need to talk, and we also will do pretty fine without. But we do talk and what I know is you are essentially a decent and totally wonderful human being and I'll hang around a long time for you.

You dress. It's a crying shame to cover up your body. I want to hold you, want to make love with you, you know and we don't and I still feel OK. Fully dressed, midnight butterfly in this light of day, we hold each other, grind, baby, grind so I could take a chunk out of your neck by way of breakfast.

I drive you home. Wish I had a primrose-yellow

Hispano-Suiza, with a chauffeur to take *you* home. Stop the car.

You kiss me, your lips so tender and sensuous I don't want to go. So what else is new? I release my safety belt to hold you, dangerous ground, ground where my feet have wings of flame.

Is it OK, you say, are you really pissed off that I have to get home?

Well, now, my dear, I hadn't thought of that. Am I pissed off? No, I'm not. Tell you if I was I wouldn't see you. Which is true. Actually true. Goddawmighty! Lady Jay the Impetuous discovers an instinct for a smidgeon of dignity!

So I drive back, pig out on a hi-cal breakfast, devour Sunday paper trash, wander home, hug the pillow you lay on, find a blonde hair or two, grin like an idiot, realise my hangover's gone, work like a trooper all afternoon, sip a little brandy come early evening, and raise my glass to your very good health.

my *dear* Dionne . . .

CHAPTER SEVENTEEN

In fact, there were signs of ending and unease in what she had written. Dumb shit, Jay, always wise after the non-event! And why had she and Dionne never fallen In Love? Perhaps it would have been too easy: they'd made love the first night they met, both involved with women who gave them pain. Then on, they'd got it on from time to happy time, eaten together every week, seen movies, theatre, films, drag, done disco, reggae, boogie . . . Why not fall in love with someone you actually *like* and feel easy with? Jay was now In Love with the impossible Lucy, Dionne went for butch crew-cut teenagers, and they hugged each other's hurt away and made love like some people offer Kleenex and brandy in times of stress.

And after that evening when Dionne said 'it' was over, they had some undoing to go through, so near the edge of agony and ecstasy. They treated each other more carefully than friends usually do, chose each other little gifts, tiny wooden ducks from China, sprays of silk roses, jazz collectors' tapes. One time, Dionne brought Jay a huge bunch of plaited purple garlic from the Breton onion man who hung around in Islington from time to time. Jay brought Dionne honeycomb cell shaped soap and an oil and sand picture with its ever-changing magic. Treasure to the treasured. At least she and Dionne knew how precious they were to each other.

'It's a shame, dear,' said Francis. 'I hoped you two silly dykes had realised Nirvana, but here you are, alone and palely loitering for the love of your Lucy-o! And Dionne! You've seen the latest? Dear, they were down at the Paradise the other night . . . looks serious.'

No, Jay had not seen the latest.

'What's she like?'

Goddam it, yes, she was jealous. Jealous. Jealous? She wanted Dionne to have the best, oh yeah, Jay, and is that you? Just that she'd seen Dionne so often sad and unsure. And laughing and ecstatic in her arms. And the bloody rest of it.

'Well, dear,' said Francis, considering, 'she must be at least — twelve? Head to toe black leather, and I believe she has a ring through her nose. Which is considered a sign of beauty in certain parts of the globe. The little mouth was born with a scowl, the brows positively

beetle over the turned-up be-ringed breathing appara-
tus. And Dionne is enraptured.'

'Sounds like a clone of Studs,' said Jay. Studs had
been Dionne's last Big Romance. She'd moved in on
and in with Dionne, spitting scorn at her friends,
slurring drunk at parties. Jamie called her Ug the
Cavewoman, Francis had tried talking with her on
many occasions:

'Only I do find monosyllables wearing, dear!'

Dionne went for the outlaw type, or so she said, then
mothered and civilised them until they were unrecog-
nisable, and when her dream of civilised and raunchy
equality went out the slammed door, there she was
alone again, smoking a little more than usual, drinking
a little more than necessary and swearing herself to
celibacy until the next sulky brow slouched into view
and stole her hopeful heart away. And this one Francis
named Piggy-wig.

Jay visited the new ménage. Piggy-wig was in the
kitchen, Dionne opened a bottle of white wine and they
sat in the elegant grey-blue lounge. Crashes and curses
off stage.

'Do join us, Sandy,' called Dionne.

'Can't work your fucking washing machine, can I?'
said Piggy-wig, gulping lager in the doorway and
strutting out again.

'At least you're not doing her washing,' said Jay.
'Cheers!'

'And how's Lucy?' said Dionne.

'Touché,' said Jay. 'Well, we're meeting next week,
hopefully to really get this show on the road. We had
lunch the other day. Even held hands over coffee.'

*'I feel I'm free-falling, Jay,' said Lucy, her hand light
and warm in Jay's. 'I don't know what's happening.'*

'You think I do?' said Jay.

And their eyes met.

Saint Jay re-adjusted her halo as the Queen of Heaven drove away.

'What's this?' said Piggy-wig, straddling a chair with the triumph of one who has mistressed a Zanussi automatic. The finishing touch would have been brylcreem only she was wearing it anyway.

'Jay's In Love with an impossible woman,' said Dionne conversationally.

'Straight?' said Piggy-wig.

'So far,' said Jay. She had no wish to discuss Lucy around this stranger.

'How long have you been in love then?'

'Oh, about three months,' said Jay lightly. Five months, three weeks, four days . . . None of your goddam business!

'I couldn't put up with that,' said Piggy-wig. 'Three months! What's her sign?'

'Gemini,' said Jay.

Piggy-wig shook her head knowingly.

'You'd better jump on her.'

'*I'm* Gemini, Sandy,' said Dionne.

'That's what I mean, babe.'

This time she grinned. Jay suddenly saw: there was a pixie smile in the tough young eyes. Underneath all the leatherado, she was shy as hell and pleased as Punch with Dionne. Sandy. Not Piggy-wig. Friends can never love each other's lovers, but if our friends are happy? So be it.

'I'm off up the pub, babes,' said Sandy, ruffling Dionne's hair. 'Let you two have a good old gossip. Bye.' She bent and kissed Dionne and slammed out of the flat.

'Isn't she sweet?' said Dionne.

'Hard work, Dionne.'

'And Lucy's easy?'

CHAPTER EIGHTEEN

For Jay, many things in life had been easy, a walk-over;
she had leapt over and through the academic hurdles
and hoops of childhood and teenage with a lazy facility
that she only realised later. Sailed through college,
picked up academic jargon like a duckling gobbles
worms.

No, Lucy was not easy and so she loved her. Or: she
loved Lucy and so she was not easy; she was not at
ease.

For their next meeting, the enticing mirage of a
global exhibition fuelled by their energy, she slowed
down and prepared a seduction dinner. Just in case.
Glamorous food was a challenge she had set herself
and won.

Grating ginger, Phoebe Snow on the stereo *thank you
but I'm just lookin'*, sipping wine, a wry smile damping
her forest fire, she thought, at least we'll have a good
meal. Good? Jay was into labour-intensive food for The
Beloved. Only this beloved never seemed to notice.

Jay summed up for herself.

Kissing was OK. Usually.

Both she and Lucy seemed to have some kind of
thing for breasts.

Hum.

That was all she *knew* about Lucy sexually.

So far.

Oh, to hell and be spontaneous! She concentrated on
the culinary. She knew what to do there.

First there was Caribbean sea-food, a trip to Brixton,

fresh limes, hand-ground spices, fresh coriander, hot-juiced ginger, a sloosh of Barbados rum.

Shoppin' in endless malls, waitin' for phone calls . . .

She changed Phoebe Snow for Fela Anakupalo Kuti, a dive into Desmond's Hip City . . .

Then came a salad, forty luscious shades of biting green and purple, roasted sesame seeds, toasted sunflower seeds, walnut oil and red wine vinegar. And hazelnut stuffed aubergines, mozzarella cheese, parmesan, the tiniest button mushrooms she could find.

Zombie no go unless you tell im to go

The Communards.

And then meringues, liqueur whipped cream and crushed raspberries from Andalucia.

Pretty damn good, Jay!

And she had laid in Greek brandy and pink champagne for old times' sake. *Her* fond memories anyway, and what did Lucy think? Would she ever know?

Maybe next time you'll wear a pink carnation / so I can recognise you – hooo!

Said Sarah Jane Morris.

Ding-dong, said the bell.

Licketty-split, said Jay's feet.

Boom-bang-a-bang-boooooooom! said Jay's heart.

Come on in! said Jay.

Lucy's mood had rallied. Her eyes were sparkling, cheeks flushed, body clad in a sea-green that lit the depths of her eyes, her beautiful eyes. And she produced a sheaf of exhibition papers with a flourish; she'd even written some of the wording to go under the photos. Neat and brilliant! And she loved the stills Jay had dug out; her lovely lips tasted the Melina Mercouri and she raised her glass to Jay. The air relaxed to Pergolesi, Purcell, Bach.

Work raced by like a thrilling dirt-track race, food finished with relish and grace, they sat holding hands, warmth flowing like the water in a fantastic Escher waterfall. Kissed very gently. Ms Piggy-wig, Sandy the winner, had said *jump on her!* Hah! What did she know, rhapsodised Jay into Lucy's neck. Be cool, be natural. But as they sank to the floor, naturally, Jay sensed a tension in Lucy. Easy, she told herself, easy.

Lucy sat up abruptly and lit a cigarette.

'Sorry,' she said, 'I just . . .'

'Need some time?' said Jay, sure and warm like her heartbeat.

'Mm.'

'Darling,' said Jay, 'if time is what we need, let's take it. Let's do that weekend, Lucy. I want time with you. You know it. I believe you want it too. Get your goddam diary and let's make a date.'

'I don't have my diary with me,' said Lucy, sipping wine and suddenly distracted.

Jay sighed from her guts. What was it? Did Lucy think of herself as that heterosexually convenient phenomenon, the 'non-orgasmic woman'; had sex been awful for her? *Jump on her!* How the hell do you jump on a Lucy, a lady, a Lucy, someone who appears fragile as glass, goes warm and soft like a trusting animal in your arms, then tough as steel with her polished NO — ?

'Do you *want* to have a weekend with me? I feel sort of fixed that it would be the best thing . . . you know it would.'

In a rush, Lucy said: 'I came here tonight hoping you'd got over me.'

'What? Got over you? I can never get over you, Lucy. I love you.'

Lucy held her close. Christ, thought Jay. I'm paralysed. But galvanised herself in the heat to tease away Lucy's shirt, work her jeans loose, kneaded her stomach, breathe fire into her breasts.

Lucy buried her face in Jay's neck, moaned into her mouth.

'I love you, Jay,' she said, voice breaking on 'you'. 'There you are, I've said it. I love you.'

'I'm so glad,' whispered Baby Jay, cherub wings fluttering rose-pink ecstasy, 'So glad. Darling. Let's go to bed.'

'No. I have to go home,' said Lucy, as if torn.

'Why?' said Jay wildly. 'Why? Your damn son?'

'No, I have to be up early in the morning.

'I don't understand,' said Jay. 'I just don't understand.'

She pulled away and gave herself some time rolling and lighting a cigarette. Lucy's hand moved through her hair and she clenched her teeth against the tantalising sensation.

'Jay, you're shaking,' she said.

'Sexual arousal, darling,' said Jay, brittle, agonised.

'And you're a woman,' said Lucy — wonderingly?

'Yeah, lady. I'm a woman and so are you. Lucy?'

It was going to be sheer pain to say it, but acid agony to hold it in.

'Yes?' Lucy's hand was shaky against her cheek.

'If I was a man, I believe you'd be having an affair with me. Is that true?'

Lucy said nothing. Her hand was still.

'Because if it is, you really should look at that,' said Jay, letting the slow words hold her terror. 'You really should. Give us some time. A weekend — we both work, there's no time in the week. I don't want to rush this. For chrissake, you said you love me. Say it. What am I supposed to do? Jump on you?'

Oh, shit! Lucy was crying. Oh oh oh oh SHIT!

'Darling, Lucy, I'm sorry, darling,' said Jay, 'but I'm this bloody dyke, dear, oh dear Lucy, I don't understand.'

'Just I know you've been busy and enjoying your

friends. I've been really glad about that. Maybe I'm not the one for you.'

Distractions, distractions, squirt chilli juice in a wounded elephant's eye . . .

'Lucy, for the love of God,' said Jay, 'it's *you*. You. I want you. I love you. Stay with me. Now, And if you can't right now, then come away with me. Give us a chance. You know you want to.'

'I don't know what to do,' said Lucy, hiding her face, tears pouring through her clenched fingers. 'You'll have to decide for both of us.'

'OK,' said Jay, wrapping her arms around Lucy, suddenly so tiny, 'I'll tell you. If you have to go home now, and I wish you wouldn't, then call me tomorrow and give me a date. OK?'

'I'll call you tomorrow,' said Lucy, then she whispered, 'Only I may not be able to give you a date.'

Jay wanted to say *then don't bother calling*.

But she didn't have the nerve.

And she drunk herself to sleep. No more thoughts.

And Lucy called her in the morning, swept away all doubts with a rush of enthusiasm about the exhibition, and only when they'd hung up did Jay realise that she hadn't given her a date, a time; that she — *they*? — were just where they'd been five months before. She was richer only by stolen kisses and the rhapsody her tongue had played over Lucy's breasts.

CHAPTER NINETEEN

'How were Dionne and Piggy-wig?' said Francis, yawning over the first coffee of the day.

'Her name's Sandy,' said Jay shortly. From time to time she had to pull him up. Because he never meant bitchiness, because he was kind like all good people who've been hurt, he never minded.

'Sorry, darling. I stand corrected. She's got the seal of approval, I take it?'

'Oh, Francis, shut up. She's OK. I wouldn't choose her, but then I'm not exactly the legend of taste and discretion.'

Sometimes, like now, she wondered if Francis knew what it was be in love. His raptures over pretty strangers and their come-hither designer clothes were as over-the-top as his enthusiasm for a new cocktail. She looked at him.

'OK, Mr Tolerance, sorry yourself. I'm just an old bitch. But, Francis, seriously, have you ever been In Love, like a big one?'

'Darling,' he said, folding one long leg over the other, sweeping his glasses to the desk, 'I have been in love most of my life. As to "a big one", dear, what a thing to say to an ageing queen! I suppose you mean an all-consuming I-will-do-anything-for-you passion? Is Lucy giving you more of a hard time? She's terribly good at it, isn't she? Dare I say give it up? That phrase rings in my dyke agony uncle ears constantly. Wasted on you of course.'

But Jay wanted more.

'Come on, Francis, you've side-stepped my question with your habitual élan, it's confession time. Francis In Love.'

Francis lit a cigarette.

'Honey, don't let me *commence*! As Saint Truman Capote says — do you know that story? One of his marvellous women, when anyone asks her anything about herself, she just rolls out that line... *Honey, don't let me commence*! It says it all. I was madly in love once, darling. And for a while, so was he. We were very à deux, and I was the hoover and windolene queen. I would not let him eat anything canned or frozen, I spoilt him to pieces. I was down the market every day with my shopper, dear, for veg. I can spot a cheap cauli at a hundred paces. Oh, it was heaven.'

'And?'

'Oh, isn't she a prurient little dyke, pull—ease!' he said, rolling his eyes. 'Well, it went off. Just that. He wanted an open relationship after a while which meant him bringing bits of trade back and then saying couldn't we be just sisters? I am a jealous, possessive sodden Kleenex style bitch when in love. I did not feel sisterly. He left.'

'What about now? I mean, you should be with someone wonderful.'

'Thank you so much. Well, darling, I do want to be In Love. Of course I do. What else is there? But I'm not exactly a chicken any more, dear. I am rapidly turning into a ghastly old queen ogling rent boys. The day they expect me to pay for it, I shall retire. In Love, in love, Oh Love! I'm just rather despairing about it happening. I want it to. I live in hope. I'd adore it, but time is fleeting. I refuse to sit at home with my needlepoint, dear. Meanwhile, I take what I can get: safe sex with a bit of clean trade. I'm not proud. Miss Proud left home with my Big Romance. It's better than nothing.'

'Hum,' said Jay, *at least that way you don't get your heart broken.*

'Well, hmm, Camille?'

'Let's go have a drink,' said Jay. 'It's five to eleven.'

In the pub, red plush and genteel fake gas globes, Francis loaded the juke box.

'Since you appear to be doing a thesis on True Romance,' he said, smiling.

'Country and Western, Francis?'

'Get the lyrics, dear!'

I done bought her a di'mond ring,
An' a purdy rose-trimmed hat,
Sat out under th' moonlight,
Kissin' an' huggin' an' all of that,
An' yuh know whut she done,
Gone an' ended mah fun – ?
She took my heart and squashed the sucker flat.

'There you have it,' said Francis, 'so eloquent. And now let us pass on to Lucy — we have forty minutes until Happy Hour.'

Jay giggled as Patsy Cline went *walkin' after midnight, searchin' for yee-ew!*

'Honey, don't let me *commence*!' she said.

CHAPTER TWENTY

More days and weeks went by. This year seemed to be full of them. These sun and moon hour and minute and second sections of time. Went by. Went by without Lucy, each dark and light portion of time acquired a date and name only when they met. For example: June 7th, midday, or June 5th, 5.30. To focus still further, corridor of work and car park. Duration of meaningful contact, two and a half minutes, fifteen minutes. Yo, Jay, have yourself a wallow!

Lucy was treating Jay like a delightful new acquaintance she couldn't quite place or fit into her life. Jay cursed that she was so pleased with the crumbs of comfort: coffee, a drink, a phonecall. Almost a month went by before she allowed herself an evening to realise that there was at the very least and latest, an unfinished conversation between them. And Lucy was blithely or otherwise ignoring that fact.

Lucy couldn't find time to come over for an evening; the globally significant exhibition was floating on some remote iceberg; Jeremy had an agent, an opening; Lucy's sister was ill and needed her (Jay recalled Lucy's exasperated indifference to her sister); the painters were coming. Busy busy busy.

GODDAM IT! If you want to see someone, none of these things stand in the way!

Thought Jay.

For the first time, she turned Lucy down for lunch. She would not be squeezed in. Or out.

When Lucy suggested a quick drink, Jay was cut to the quick and described herself, with sparse and ironic regret, as 'working late'.

And was out every night, so much that Lucy actually said: *I've called you!*, her glorious eyes questioning, troubled green, burning brown.

'Been busy,' said Jay.

'You're still angry with me, Jay. Look, there's lot of things I just can't handle.'

Won't.

'Let's talk,' said Lucy.

Jay toyed with being busy. Again. Easy enough to fill her empty time, time without love, without Lucy. She looked polite.

'How about next Wednesday,' said Lucy. 'I'll come over about six. I'll have to go at nine.'

How convenient.

'Mm,' she said, wordless at how she couldn't spit out that furious NO! At Art College, she'd had a friend whose catch phrase when asked for a date, was: How about next July, I seem to have a Wednesday free. Oh, to be flip, oh not to care!

For that evening — *Yah! three lousy hours!* — she laid in white wine and gin. Before, during, after. She lived in hope and dread.

We have to *talk?*

Hmmmmmmmmmmm.

Since Lucy had said it, then let her talk. Jay had poured a million words her way with little response. Let *Lucy* articulate, lay herself on whatever uncomfortable line it was that she had elected to draw. Just for once.

Enter Lucy, pale, tight-jawed, polite, smile not reaching her eyes.

Two glasses of wine.

Pouring rain and flat grey sky outside.

Did Lucy sense? What did Lucy sense? What was the sense? Jesus, what was this aching nonsense?

Well, said Lucy.

We—ell, drawled Jay.

We are not going to have an affair, said Lucy, hand shaking a little on her cigarette. She gulped wine and set her glass down firm as a full stop. Period, full stop, as Dionne would say.

Jay trembled and clamped her teeth together on a chill sip of wine, the kiss of alcohol meaningless on the tight-lipped blues.

She felt cornered, counted out by this cool precision, fighting for something which had given every sign of gracious flowering . . . *from time to time.* She forced herself to admit the words. But no less for that? Surely?

'Look,' she said, unable to meet Lucy's eyes, then unable to look away, 'you kissed me. More than once. Didn't you *like* that?'

'Yes, yes,' said Lucy, as if brushing ash from her skirt. 'But that's got nothing to do with it . . .'

She took a tight breath and stared at her knee. Then said, as if reading from an autocue:

'I am not going to have an affair with you. We're working together now, there's the exhibition and all those projects, Jay.'

'Don't you want to?'

'I'm not going to. It's my decision. It's nothing to do with you.'

Oh, God, thought Jay, I can't bear it. Maybe for ten years would be better than no. And she *knew* how urgent and fervent their kisses had been, how close Lucy had been to abandoning whatever it was that held her back, made her withhold her beautiful body. *I cannot bear it.* I will not take no unless I know she really means it, as strongly as she kissed me.

'I really don't want to close this off,' she said, grinding her cigarette to ash and frayed tobacco. 'I've kissed you and more, and none of that lightly, and you *know*, and I *know*, that it would be so good — for Chrissake,' she said. 'Screw all that work and exhibition shit, I want *you.*'

'I was afraid you'd say that,' said Lucy, 'Oh, God.'

Oh shit, thought Jay.

'But it's true,' she said aloud, forcing her eyes to focus on the middle distance. 'I've got a job. In perpetuo, as Francis says, if only because no one else would be fool enough to do it. I'm only doing the other stuff to be with you. A job is a job. You sell your time for money to have a better time in the unsold hours. Lucy, I'm in love with you like I've never been with anyone before. No one moves me like you. And you . . . you're sitting there breaking my fucking heart.'

She bit back the unwordable sweet pain of when Lucy had whispered: *I love you, I love you, there you are* . . . And what had she said, stunned by her apocalyptic vision of lovely Lucy, Lucy in love with her? From another life, she heard herself: *I'm so glad, so glad.*

She put her head on the table and wept. Jay with no ace in the hole. Death Row. No stay of execution. She heard Lucy's chair scrape and felt her arms round her shoulders. From her ice age, she wrenched herself to turn and wrap both arms round Lucy's waist, her pounding head butting against the soft silk of her blouse. *Hold tight*, said Lucy, suddenly mummy. Jay gripped, burrowed her head in Lucy's belly: here so safe and wanted inside her beloved Jeremy had grown; her brow nudged Lucy's breasts, where Jeremy had sucked himself full and strong, where she had found a contentment warm as summer wind across white sands; here she had swum easy as a seal, crystal seas halcyon over her head. She trembled at the razor-sharp sleet of misery: losing Lucy.

Lucy's firm small hand cupped her chin and drew her face upwards. Those eyes, troubled and wet, those eyes, Lucy's glorious eyes.

Jesus, thought Jay, I must look a mess, careful enhancing make-up at the school of Cherry Morello smeared everywhere. And this mess of me is what I want her to love. God, I'm doing this all wrong, I've done all this wrong.

Lucy's beautiful face was agonised. She sat down again, poured herself and Jay more wine; it flooded Jay's mouth and throat, cloying, choking like foul water.

'I know you're in love with me,' said Lucy, making a neat mound of cigarette ash, firming her hand against shaking, 'and I said it before, and I'll say it here and now. I do love you. I'm not *in love* with you — there's a difference.'

Yeah, thought Jay, as if wading through cement, let's be semantic, let's forget the way our eyes met, the way our bodies clung so hungrily together.

Lucy said:

'I just don't want to mess up your life. I want you to make something of it. I don't want you to drop this exhibition, think what it could do for you. And all these projects — you could really go places.'

'I know,' said Jay. 'I don't give a goddam. I want to be your lover. And I believe you *want* that as well. I know you're scared of it, fuck it, you said you felt safe with me. And have I ever pushed you? Have I?'

Suddenly she was furious and jabbed out:

'And I'll mess up my own life if I want to, that's not your problem. I didn't ask to fall in love with you, but by God, lady, I have, and I have every reason to believe you want to as well.'

'I am not going to,' said Lucy vehemently. 'Don't you understand? I'm trying to be clear. And this is my decision. For me. I want to be honest. I came here to try and be clear with you. I could have said anything, made an excuse, but I wanted to be straight and it's only making things worse.'

Lucy wept, her hand against her face, wiped her eyes as more tears came. Jay so wanted to make it better, but how? With the awfulness of Lucy crying, still she was furious.

Goddam it to hell, lady, you've been straight all your life. I am the only woman you've felt like this about, the only woman you've kissed and caressed this way. And you're forty something and straight and divorced and celibate and a mother and I couldn't have found a more complicated situation to fall in love with. And I bet no man has ever appreciated the lava flow of sensuality so near your ice-perfect surface.

Jay'd had enough men to know they treat a woman's body with anything from contempt and rage to inept uncertainty and fear; once in a blue moon only, with real fascination and tenderness. But there's never the sure intuition that lies between women, welds them together. Like home, like the home you dream of, where people accept you and love you just the way you are. She knew with her first woman, when she was twenty. And Lucy was forty something... no! She put a clamp on thinking into Lucy's whys and wherefores. Let there be an end to this self-searching monologue. Let Lucy say for herself what was on her mind.

'I'm so sorry,' she said, 'sorry you're crying.'

'You're crying too,' said Lucy. 'It's just I see all this pain and shit, and it's all my fault.'

'Bullshit,' said Jay gently, and put her arms round Lucy's shoulders. 'Bullshit. There's two of us here.'

'I'm forty-eight,' said Lucy.

'So fucking what?' said Jay. 'You said you felt like a teenager when you kissed me.'

'*NO! LISTEN TO ME!* I'm forty-eight. I have a career. I have a highly talented son who, right or wrong, I have committed myself to. It's just not going to work.'

You have a lot to lose, thought Jay, rolling a cigarette, and you know damn well you might have to, or at least turn it all upside down if you let yourself fall in love with me.

'I still think you'd be having an affair with me if I was a man,' she said.

'Jay, you're a very seductive woman,' said Lucy.

'Not seductive enough, obviously,' said Jay.

'What do you mean?'

'Well, why aren't you seduced?'

'Jay, Jay, it's not that. It's not you. It's me. Why don't you find someone else?'

'Who? Who else is there? It's you I want, you turn me on, darling.'

Lucy managed a laugh shattered like a dropped mirror.

'Christ,' she said, 'What a pair. At least we can laugh. I don't know why I'm laughing.'

Jay laughed too, but unease and bitterness slammed a full stop and left her chill and foolish.

'Desperation, I guess,' she said, 'because I'm only too aware that you're going soon, back to play happy families with Jeremy. There's never any time, Lucy, you've got to give it real time. I don't accept this No, I just don't believe you.'

'Well, oh God, Jay, you're a hard woman.'

'I know,' said Jay, irony permitting a hah! of laughter. 'They don't call me bitch for nothing. I've worked for this title. Lucy — give *us* a weekend.'

'I just don't know,' said Lucy.

'Well, I do,' said Jay. 'Marry me, Lucy, eh?'

'I've been married,' said Lucy.

''Samatter with you? You don't do things twice? Marry me.'

She knew all at once that the measured time, the false normality of banter, everything led to an end she dreaded. Lucy stood to go.

'I'm aware that I'm leaving you on your own,' she said. 'Like you said, happy families. What will you do when I'm gone, back to my safe life?'

As if she cared!

'Get drunk,' said Jay crudely. 'Who gives a shit.'

'I'll make you some tea,' said Lucy.

Mother I don't need — the one who brought me up cost a lot in therapy to get over.

'I won't drink it,' said Jay, tears gushing hot down her

cheeks. 'I'm going to get drunk, to hell, I've been half drunk half my life, who gives a fuck if I'm drunk again? At least that way I can stop thinking, words bloody words.'

Lucy made tea. Jay sat back and crossed her arms.

'Drink it yourself,' she said, forcing the words out. 'I said I didn't want it.'

She sloshed more wine into her glass. Fucking bottle was empty. She opened the other bottle — fake champagne and nothing to celebrate. She filled Lucy's glass. Go, bitch, go! She could about stagger to the off-licence and obliterate the rest of the evening.

'I have to leave,' said Lucy, but sat and drank, sat and lit a cigarette, sniffed away more tears.

'Look, Jay,' she said, 'I hate to go and leave you in this state.'

'So stay.'

'I can't.'

'So go.'

'Look. It's all so sudden for me. Just give it time. I need some space and time. Just leave it for a while.'

Jay's ears rung with the words. A reprieve! Cool water in the parched circles of hell. God, if it was just time! You can't make love at pistol point . . . her being filled with remorse, and she checked herself from flinging her arms round Lucy: steady, Jay, she told herself, we're only seconds away from no, nay, never.

'OK,' she said and they managed a shaky hug at the door.

Time.

' . . . *after all, time is a great healer . . .*'

Camp screen love courtesy of Judy Garland and Clark Gable. And her mind tried to blank out the rest of it. But the Hollywood words rolled on.

' . . . *and as I speed through the dark night to the abyss of oblivion, I can only say thanks, thanks for the memory . . .'*

I cried for you.

She propped up the champagne blurred photo of Lucy at her birthday. Lucy laughing, smoking, Lucy with Jamie's feather boa round her shoulders, Lucy who had kissed her.

Lucy looked straight into the camera with a look she had taken — and still, against the odds — with a look Jay thought of as love.

CHAPTER TWENTY-ONE

Giving it time, Jay thought, is not enough. Not good enough to fret the days away; let her use them, enjoy, let there be something rich about her to love and desire. Having wrested from Lucy an *I don't know, you'll have to decide for both of us,* having an 'us' acknowledged, she felt there was a purpose to this time of denial. Moments of doubt she magicked away with the spell of Lucy's eyes. Jesus! Were they ever professional, boy, did they ever work hard, well, *didn't* they just talk and work as if that melodrama of near separation had never happened.

Francis was delighted with Jay's wild renewed enthusiasm for the magazine.

'I really did think you'd gone, dear,' he said. 'You've been like a YTS trainee for the past millennia. Dragged off the dole queue and hating every minute. But then I realised you had joined the queue of dolour — I take it from your sparkling eyes that Lucy's dropped her drawers and flung herself into sapphic bliss?'

Jay winced.

'Actually, no,' she said. 'We — I stress 'we' — we're giving it some real space and time.'

'Oh no!' said Francis, raising his eyes to the peeling ceiling. 'I do apologise! How gross of me! Well, who is it, darling? Do tell. *Who* is the lucky dyke putting the roses into your cheeks?'

Jay kissed the top of his head.

'It's Lucy,' she said, smiling. 'Ad infinitum. I'm nothing if not consistent. But I realised I'd been a bit heavy. She needs time.'

'You treat her far too well, darling. I mean, you've done the prelims, dear, in your own inimitable fashion — roses, champagne, adoration, necking and fumbling. Forgive me for assuming my role of dyke agony uncle once more, but really, lovey! How much bloody time does she need? Our Titian Lucy isn't exactly virgo intacta. Unless Jem-boy was an immaculate conception . . .?'

Jay hated the way he came out with things she whisked to the edges of her mind.

'Come on, Francis, what about if you were forty some and straight and never kissed a man before? And suddenly there was a rampant little queen dying to violate everything you've thought of as normal?'

'Sounds like heaven! No, I can't imagine it. But men and women are utterly different. Especially sexually. With a man it's like a rocket: it fires and goes into orbit or it crashes. You know pretty soon. But I've talked, as you know, to so many women, and sex seems to be a wholly *other* experience. Would you care to hear my analogy?'

'Go ahead,' said Jay, enjoying this objective discussion where she could focus entirely on the delirium and dilemma of Lucy.

'Right. You know when you go on a swing when

you're a child — one of those municipal swings. And then you twist round and round? Slowly, because the chain gets heavier and heavier? And then you lift your feet off the ground and rush round and round, faster and faster and the momentum even twists the chain up again the other way?'

Jay closed her eyes, Jesus, yeah!

'I know.'

'Well, your Lucy has got you winding her chain, darling, and she just won't take her feet off the ground and let go — am I right?'

'I guess.'

'Jay, she might never let go. Those exquisite hand-tailored shoes would not feel that their place is in an airy whirl of orgasmic delight. But no one else has ever even wound up that chain. If she does let go with anyone, it'll be you. But she might never.'

Jay's heart knew better, was utterly sure, given the picture of the swing, that Lucy was poised for a recklessly brilliant let go. *LET'S GO!*

And she recalled her favourite Hans Andersen fairy-tale, the one that had brought her time and again to tears. *The Garden of Paradise.* The prince is given the freedom of the garden if only he does not kiss the fairy. The first night he looks into her bower, the second night he bends over her, and the third night he cannot resist kissing her. There is a clap of thunder and the garden disappears. For ever.

She had reason to be wary, reason to act cool. She'd almost lost her garden of paradise in heat and haste and desire. She would not make that mistake again.

CHAPTER TWENTY-TWO

But there came a point when beautiful stories and analogies wore thin. Usually at a sleepless three a.m. Jay had always said you know who you are at three a.m. Because you're always utterly alone then. There may be a lover, a friend, asleep beside you, but who is wide-eyed as a marigold in the trackless dark? Just you and you. And more and more she met herself at this hour, too late to phone anyone, too weary to sleep.

At three a.m. she was Jay-in-love-with-Lucy, writing bad poetry or self-indulgent screeds of what daylight sneered at as a journal. Some weeks she would send a dozen poems, sometimes none. All Lucy ever showed was embarrassed appreciation.

'It's beautiful, Jay. You have such talent. Don't waste it all on me.'

Waste? Jay couldn't believe her saying that. If she didn't know she was worth it, worth everything, then by God, Jay would leave her in no doubt. And she softened her demanding *when* to spending time listening to Lucy, thrilling her with music and words, filled with a need to have Lucy know she was loved unconditionally.

That was the feeling. If they'd spent a particularly warm close time together, Jay even wondered if she and Lucy could be unique friends and veer away from this sexual desire which shimmered like an uncrossable burning field for Lucy. She knew she couldn't, didn't want to. But what if — what if that's all there is? She threw out the uncomfortable question, its pain-filled answer. Here and now, just be here and now. God, what an old hippy I am, jeered Jay.

Lucy basked in the tender warmth lavished her way. She relaxed and told Jay about her life, with the wry humour of a survivor.

She had always been a self-sufficient woman, since the married years with Martin. He had bowled her over when she was seventeen and girls got married. She adored him and tied her life up totally with his. The newly-married couple on the up and up. Impromptu suppers for a dozen friends? No problem to Lucy, who kept smiling through, witty and charming, zipping through three courses of creative cuisine into a smart frock and an atomised squirt of Coty L'Amant in the time it took Martin and 'the gang' to get home.

But then at two or three after midnight, a stack of dishes in the sink promising her a greasy good morning, Martin would feel drunkenly randy and she fought first her tiredness then her (unreasonable?) anger when the next evening was the same. A million and one impressive ways with left-overs.

'Just a few of the chaps and chapesses, darling,' over the phone in the late afternoon when she had purged wine stains and ashtrays, boxed up the empties, made the kitchen immaculate yet again.

'Do we always have to?' she asked him. 'Why don't we go over to Richard and Jane's one evening? Or John and Siobhan's?'

This was 3.30 a.m., Martin nuzzling her exhausted neck.

'Life in the fast lane, sweetheart,' he said. 'And you do it so well. Anyway, you're at home all day.'

'And Jane works? Siobhan *works*?' Lucy was enraged.

'Lucy, come *on*,' said Martin, fumbling her breasts.

'No,' said Lucy, needing a cuddle, to be heard, to sleep.

'Oh, fuck you!' shouted Martin, and stomped off to the spare room.

In the morning, Lucy feigned sleep. That evening brought a repentant young husband, flowers and wine, an evening to themselves. Martin even cooked, every pan in the place, 'nothing too good for *my* wife!' He was so pleased with himself, so sure she'd forgive the little boy sorry-and-lost-without-her. After a few scotches, he told her he'd buy a dishwasher, throwing in a string of fatuous clichés about her delicate hands, sparkling and making her laugh. Around ten, Lucy felt mellow, even tender. Moved towards him. Kissed him.

'Atta girl,' said he, dialling numbers. 'Feeling better? We should just make it to the cabaret — everyone's there. Some people I have to meet, you'd love them. Sling on something gorgeous!'

'You go,' said Lucy. 'I'll be fine.'

And he went. If she was sure? She was sure.

'He went?' said Jay, incredulous.

'Yup,' said Lucy, nearly thirty years on, lighting a cigarette, tossing away a cloud of smoke with the word.

It got worse.

Over the months, she found Martin couldn't have sex sober. And then, when she knew she didn't want to have sex with him at all, she was pregnant. A traumatic birth brought wonder boy Jeremy. Martin was so delighted at the idea of fatherhood that he became lovely and loving again, even drank less. Anything for the mother of his son!

All this came from Lucy in a rush, as if she was giving the background to someone else's story.

'Don't stop there,' said Jay, pouring wine and beginning to understand why Jeremy was so precious, to be redeemed from his traumas and late-night binges even at the age of twenty-five.

'Well, I decided I wanted a divorce. And I wanted my

son. So I nudged Martin in the direction of a mindless blonde divorcee. The dangerous type. Big tits and lipstick. He thought he was having a secret affair, and everyone thought I didn't know and was terribly sympathetic. Oh, poor Lucy! Poor Lucy? I was getting what I wanted. Very firmly on the pill, Jay. He was heavily into sex with me during his affair, he felt so guilty.'

'Hold on,' said Jay. 'I thought he'd reformed to be a daddy. You sound so definite. Did you just fall out of love, or what?'

Lucy lit another cigarette, drank her wine, and her voice came out as if she was reading a script.

'He had been very *good* while I was pregnant. I told him sex could damage the baby. But when Jem was born, there was no reason I could give him why not. I just didn't want to. But we were married, conjugal rights, it was the fifties, Jay, men had to have sex for their health and they couldn't stop once they were turned on. There *was* a last straw. Huh. I'd had stitches after Jeremy. Ripped apart and so on. But I sure wasn't pregnant. No baby to damage. So — after I was home, four days later? a week? he had to have sex.'

'Jesus!' said Jay. 'On a scar? An unhealed scar?'

'Honey, it hurt,' said Lucy as if she was joking, 'and went septic. Back to hospital and you must restrain yourself, old boy, nudge wink. Bla bla. This is a dreary conversation, Jay.'

'Sorry,' said Jay, 'just I want to know everything about you.'

'You're sweet,' said Lucy, stroking her face, holding her hand, 'but it was a long long time ago. I even meet him for dinner from time to time. Have a laugh. Most odd, dinner with your ex-husband. We talk about Jeremy. Oh, Martin's got his fertile pin-up. She's a whizz in the kitchen. Three children they have. Can't be bad in bed either.'

Jay held her. Hug the hurt away.

'No, it's all right, Jay,' said Lucy. 'I've been over it for years.'

Then why, thought Jay, rubbing her thumb on Lucy's shoulder blades, why does your jaw tighten as you speak, why are your eyes flooded with pain? Oh, darling, she pledged, let me love you, and I will never give you pain!

Another time, Lucy talked about Jeremy, his father's wastrel shadow ever in the background. Martin had been one of the post-war most-likely-to-succeed Oxbridge brigade. Feted as a genius at twenty-one, wined and dined for his striking originality, the world his oyster and a nice vivacious wife to boot . . .

'Jeremy has his talent plus,' said Lucy. 'And the plus is me. Good old mum. I just hope to God it doesn't all go to his head and burn him out. They're sharks in the art world. That's why I like your end of it, OK, no one makes a million, but they keep producing. After I divorced Martin, the big blonde tugged strings and he became consultant designer for a detergent manufacturer. He was one of the first to design TV campaigns: you know, the super-hero voice advising the daffy housewife how she can best clean his clothes? It's a formula now. He could always sell things. He's doing pop videos now and making stars of the pretty, the talentless, the bizarre. It's all so easy for him, perhaps that's why he squandered his talent — he never had that period of garret starvation that seems to foster genius.'

'Well, Jeremy doesn't exactly slum it,' said Jay.

'Oh, shut up, Jay, forgive a mother her blind spots. I swear I have a Jewish ancestry! If he lived in squalor, I'd be round there with chicken soup and clean shirts!'

'You're very good at taking care of people,' said Jay. She'd heard Lucy at meetings, fielding worries, steering the conversation around the reefs and sandbanks of ego and uncertainty.

'No, I'm not!' said Lucy. 'Just my son. I'm no one else's mother!'

And Jay, who was no one's mother nor wanted to be, found herself mothering Lucy. Another side of love. Making lunch for Lucy and Francis, giving her lifts here and there when her car was off the road, calling her just to see how she was, ordering her home when she looked exhausted, plying her with remedies if she had a cold, rubbing her back if she was tense. Lucy's eyes lit up with warmth when she saw her. Wow, Jay was having fun! She felt beautiful, needed, and alone she dared admit to feeling loved.

CHAPTER TWENTY-THREE

And just as she was feeling sure and secure, a smile becoming a real part of her as she gloried in the feeling growing between them, Lucy gave her to understand that she was going away for three weeks. Gave her to understand. Gave her the facts to make of what she would; and make of them what she could, Jay did not understand. A cultural tour with the genius son. Murals on Mynos, pots on Paros, icons on Ios. She blanked out the sudden picture of white sands and her and Lucy in a scented olive-grove evening . . . her heart panted to slake its thirst with dreaming, but she slammed the scenes of happiness as illusion, mirage.

Which they were.

Weren't they — if Lucy could roll out this announcement like she might show a friend a new carpet.

All the build up of delight shrivelled and stripped Jay to lonely self-scourging. Fool. Fool. Fool.

What was going on? What about this time and space? She felt she'd lived a zillion eternities, crossed endless lifeless galaxies, bearing her solitude, waiting for US, waiting for the fulfilment of all that lay between them.

'Perhaps we could have lunch before you go?' she forced out, as if the idea was merely spur of the moment, merely friendly, merely pleasant.

And Lucy *would* like that, she described her itinerary over gazpacho, her beach clothes throughout a pasta salad, Jeremy's elaborate packing as she sipped brandy. Jay stuck to white wine and soda, fearing the fragile floodgates on her anger and pain.

'We must do something about this exhibition,' Jay said, with the very English concentration of one commenting on the vagaries of the weather. Who had said: *Some countries have a climate, in England we have weather*? Thank you, brain, she thought, thanks for that suave little Jay phrase, guaranteed to raise a giggle, calm things down. It mattered as little as it seemed to matter to Lucy that they would have — yet another — three weeks apart.

Jay walked Lucy to her car. Waited for some kind of sign, a handclasp, a chaste kiss on the cheek, some sign that Lucy knew the meaning of this time and space. Lucy hopped into her car, rolled the window down — a kiss? — and said:

'Four weeks today? I'll come over and we'll get this exhibition moving. I've been so busy. Bye.'

'Dinner?' said Jay.

'Oh, don't bother with that,' said Lucy. 'I'll eat before I come.'

Jay stood frozen from head to toe and watched the car accelerate down the road. From somewhere, her hands found a diary and wrote Lucy against the date four weeks away. Date? For the first time, she felt total despair weld her to the spot. Like the Tin-Man in *The Wizard of Oz*, rigid under the apple trees, she needed oil.

Four weeks.

CHAPTER TWENTY-FOUR

'I have never known *you* be so patient, Miss Jay Goodtime!' declaimed Jamie, gluing centipede eyelashes into unlikely pools of stage make-up. 'Shall I wear the Veronica Lake or the Rita Hayworth?'

They were in a windowless hole of a dressing room, backstage of the El Paradiso — another charity, bring on the bloody drag! Dionne had ordered her to go out and forget the whole thing. This evening, Jamie would wow his rowdies to riot point and make a fast get-away in what Francis called Jay's dyke-mobile. And then to Dionne's for a late night supper.

'I'm not having you sit home swapping the blues with Sister Gin,' Dionne had told Jay. 'Come and bore the ass off your buddies, baby.'

Sandy was doing a trash all-nighter at the Scala, and Dionne met them with a cocktail shaker.

'One of those bastards kept my glove this evening,' said Jamie, mock-tragic. 'A keepsake! A fan! Another cheap bloody fan! Fourteen fucking quid fifty a pair and one of them disappears on a charity night!'

'The tribulations of being a megastar!' murmured Francis.

Dionne slung on a Dietrich tape and she and Jay escaped to the kitchen, leaving Jamie and Francis screaming along to a soul-searching Burt Bacharach number.

'A bit of role playing, my dear,' she said. 'The men can sit and camp in the lounge and we girls will slave over a hot stove. Now tell me what's frozen that gorgeous face of yours.'

Since Dionne's serious no to a casual affair, Jay had found it hard to talk to her. She shrugged.

'Well, she's pissed off with the boy for a cultural break.'

'And?'

'And? What do you mean, 'and'? Imagine Sandy just saying one morning, oh, by the way, babes. I'm going on holiday this afternoon.'

'But we are having an affair. OK, OK, sorry, Jay. You must have been heartbroken.'

'I may not be screwing Lucy,' said Jay coldly. 'But that's not my definition of the quality of love. Shit, I'm trying to talk myself out of it, it's just when I see her...'

She resented Dionne being so damn cool and objective. Had been found lacking by Dionne and it hurt. She slouched back to the living room.

'Come on, Miss Dyke,' said Jamie, 'let's have a rip-along-a-Lucy session and see if we can't shoosh you into a better frame of mind. I have met this pinnacle of sexual desire, Jay. Seemed nice enough. But it's been months, dear! And not a lot of fun . . .'

'Piss off, Jamie,' said Jay. 'I don't mean that. I just don't know what to do.'

'Given that you can't give it up, and you seem unable to scrub round it at present,' said Francis, 'what exactly have you got? Lovely platonic evenings, the odd kiss and fumble? She's a strange one, this Lucy.'

'I've always thought she was interested,' said Marina quietly, 'ever since your birthday. But. Oh, Jay, I'd have thought she'd have done it by now, if she was going to. Or broken it off.'

'Has she intimated she wants to break it off?' said Francis.

'Oh, yeah,' said Jay, 'only I wouldn't let her.'

'Stop putting yourself down,' said Francis. 'If the silly bitch says no and you get her to say maybe, whatever inimitable persuasion you used, *she* changed her mind. Unless you were threatening her life? No? Well, you can never tell with dykes.'

'What about if she does say no and sticks to it, finally?' said Dionne.

'I kill myself,' said Jay. 'Next?'

'Fine,' said Dionne, 'just checking.'

'Well, *I* think, and I use that word in its broadest sense, I think you should jump on her. At least then you'll *know*!' said Jamie.

'Do you wish to know yes or no, dear Jay?' said Francis.

'Jesus! I thought 'maybe' was OK,' said Jay. 'I know you're right, but I just can't see how I'd handle 'no'.'

'Have a bloody drink,' said Jamie. 'The trouble is, Miss Galahad, this flaming green-eyed redhead has got under your skin, she's growing with you darling, like mistletoe on an oak. It's parasite time! I wish you luck, sweetie!'

'Let's talk about something else,' said Jay. 'I've got weeks to mull it over.'

'Let's play,' said Marina. 'The animal game. Come on.'

'Oh, not that old bloody chestnut!' said Jamie. 'All right. It always comes out different anyway.'

'OK,' said Marina, 'this is my version of psycho-analysis. Self-image and so on. Come on, boys and girls, drink up.'

They moved into a circle. Downed their drinks, re-filled.

'OK,' said Marina, 'who's going to start?'

'You choose,' said Jamie, 'just don't start on me!'

'Right,' said Marina, 'Dionne, what kind of animal would you be?'

Dionne flung her silky blonde head back and laughed.

'I'd be a cat,' she said, 'a platinum-blonde pedigree cat with all the refined desires of Mehitabel. I'd win blue rosettes and gorge on salmon and cream. Then I'd disappear for days and make everyone go crazy with worry while I whooped it up down the nearest alley with some ear-torn tom. No, not a tom. I guess there are lesbian cats?'

'You could start a trend, dear,' said Francis.

'Yeah. So that's me. Miss Priss on a silk cushion, yowling my bahoolas off as soon as I could run away.'

'Last time we did this you were a kitten,' said Marina. 'Are you growing up?'

'God forbid!' said Dionne, 'just that I'm living with a delinquent at the moment and it makes me feel mature.'

'Fine,' said Marina. 'Jamie?'

'Well, last time, *last* time, I was a parrot, do you remember? So long as I stuck to squawks and Pretty fucking Polly, I was fine? Well, that TV contract failed to materialise as usual, being a parrot does you fuck all in the way of good! So right now, it's obvious really, I'm a skunk. Utterly repulsive to the rest of the animal kingdom, but totally irresistible to other skunks. Fuck 'em all! Some day my stink will come!'

'Yo!' said Jay. 'And don't ask me yet. Marina, what about you?'

'I'm still some sort of bird,' said Marina. 'I thought I was a bird of paradise before, but that was in the flow of what never quite materialised — that new play? Maybe I'm an owl, watching the other owls screech down on helpless little mice, but I won't forsake my vegetarian principles. I'm a rather inept owl, really, stalking mushrooms and nuts by night.'

'Never mind,' said Jay, 'we all feel a good deal safer around you.'

'Or maybe I'm a fruitarian bat,' said Marina, laughing, 'the one that got turned down for every Drac film because she wouldn't suck blood. Swoop, swoop!'

'Is it that bad?' asked Jamie. 'My end of the theatre is deadly at the moment. Everyone's waiting for what might happen with arts subsidies. Oh, the Government hates the queers, dear. They'll starve us all to death!'

'It's fortunate that skunks and fruitarian bats have meagre appetites,' said Marina wryly. 'Francis?'

'I'm torn, dear,' he said, stretching. 'I'm a very domestic nest-building type of creature. Fanatically tidy. Which suggests a rodent of some kind. And that I'm not — a toothless harvest mouse? Did you know they're making dentures for sheep these days? Really! All the grass grinds their little molars flat. So, something nest-building. Possibly aligned to water — a sort of bank by a rushing river. Perhaps something as natty and camp as Ratty in The Wind in the Willows. Dapper, dear, Noel Coward.'

'I can see that,' said Dionne. 'Only you need to be something more lean and long-legged, my dear.'

'A whippet?' Francis raised an eyebrow. 'A whippet endlessly chasing a stuffed rabbit round a track . . . a gerbil on a wheel? God! Actually, in all semi-seriousness, knowing my penchant for warm furry places. I'd be a flea. And that would have the added advantage of being able to hop from one creature to another. And career prospects! I could join a circus and see the world!'

'Bravo!' said Marina. 'Jay?'

'Yes, you, Jay. Lighten our tone, dear,' said Francis. 'What with schizophrenic bats, isolated skunks, long-legged water rats . . . we're all verminous mutations apart from Puss here.'

'I don't know,' said Jay. 'It's a very determined little animal, whatever it is. Like an agouti: it is *going* to make its nest on *that* spot, come wind or rain, hell or high water! But it's more solid. A pig, perhaps, root root, snort, snuffle, dig in the mud and find a truffle! A rather stupid pig, I think. Rooted so deep it's in danger of the tree falling on its unknowing pig head. Yeah. I stick with a pig.'

'What a menagerie,' said Marina, draining the bottle into their glasses. 'I feel we should open a home for displaced animals.'

'What else is this place?' asked Dionne, 'or any of our places?'

'Well, that's it,' said Jamie. 'I think we've all depressed ourselves stupid. And there's no more wine. I'm going to get some beauty sleep, and wake up as a peacock!'

'You can stay if you like,' said Dionne to Jay. 'Sandy's not coming back tonight.'

'You want a surrogate pig?' said Jay.

'Yes,' said Dionne quietly. 'Just mind my pedigree claws.'

'Oh, we pigs have thick skins, Dionne, don't let the acres of pink fool you.'

'Sandy, of course, thinks I'm a bitch,' said Dionne, mouth hardening, 'wants to move in full-time, be a couple. I don't.'

'Want to talk about it?'

'Get your clothes off, Jay. No.'

They had sex wordlessly, frantically, furiously. Exhaustion.

The thing about sex, thought Jay, apart from everything else, is that for a few, for many, for countless seconds and sometimes glorious minutes, you stop thinking.

Entirely.

CHAPTER TWENTY-FIVE

Usually, Jay was studiously sober at the beginning of an evening with Lucy. Earnest and alert, edgy as hell. This time, she met Jamie in Rital's wine bar at lunchtime. Fun and laughter, a mammoth task she felt equal to.

'I mustn't get too pissed,' she said.

Jamie was looking a little fragile and they browsed through coffee and a restrained bottle of house red for the first hour. But Jay didn't want to go home for three, what, four hours to mope over Lucy, alone? And Rital, whose east European eyes had seen been and done it all for more of a century than she chose to admit, merely shrugged and locked the door.

'Houze parrr-dy, dahlink?' she said. 'Though you look like it could be a wake.'

'Champagne?' said Jay. 'You do take Access, Rital?'

'Hi take vord Hi can gehd these days!' said Rital. 'Hand ri — yid now, dear Chay, Jamie dahlink, Hi take a nap. Led yousself out!'

Jamie's mega-mouth roller-coastered Jay through side-splitting anecdotes. Jay felt lyrical, delighted. Fuck it, she thought at five, maybe I just won't go home. Do I need this Lucy? Lucy who? She wished she meant it as blithe as it sounded.

'Well, you hideous reprobate,' said Jamie, 'I have to go, plunge my flesh into the asses milk, slather on the Man Tan and hit In Chains. My public calls!'

Negotiating her way home, Jay wished she could borrow some of Jamie's crowd-quelling chutzpah to face Lucy. Lucy who didn't know she was going to be pounced on. Lucy who possibly hadn't given Jay a thought in four weeks; she certainly hadn't woken with Jay's face in her mind, slept with a dream of Jay in her arms. Or had she? Did she even know what Jay felt? Hell with it, what did the bitch know, thought Jay, trying to toughen up. Sober up, too. Jamie called three bottles of wine Betty Ford time, and commiserated on the sexual inequality of male and female livers.

'But you do have clitoral orgasms, Jay!' he said. 'Ha! *That's* sexual inequality!'

She made a huge pot of strong coffee. Pushed books and papers into piles, threw discarded clothes into the bedroom. Suddenly the door bell rang and she blessed that she'd blissed the afternoon away. She'd given more time to thinking about Lucy than anything else for months. At least the lost afternoon guaranteed a certain spontaneity. She opened the first bottle of wine, and went down to the door.

'Hi,' she said and led the way upstairs.

Lucy was the sort of redhead who bronzes beautifully. As usual she was stunning, white linen jacket and trousers supremely casual and graceful. For Jay the room was throbbing with desire. Lucy was full of her holiday and an artists' colony where Jeremy might just settle.

'And now, Jay, the exhibition,' she said, smiling.

Oh, so now we have time for the exhibition? thought Jay. Thank you SO much, Jeremy, Deo Gratias!

'Jay, what's the matter?' said Lucy.

Aside from six months of celibate desire, three bottles of wine with the greatest drag queen in the world, a won't-be-shrugged-off resentment that only *now* you sound as if you care?

'Nothing,' said Jay, staring at her foot. 'Must change the tape.'

She selected Goyescas. The music was sure as a

swing in high summer, to and fro, light as racing over a sunny lawn to the blessed shade under the trees. Up the garden path and a frisson of unease: there is no house, but a vista of a majestic lake. Stroll along its shore and find it is a seashore, primly kissed by measured trills of dippy white-capped wavelets. But dip in your toe and all at once, the waves are wild unleashed dangerous passion to sweep you off your feet, drag you around and duck you and go half-way to drown you then toss you above the tide line. Save yourself! Goyescas, where one piano plays as if there were three.

She stared at Lucy. *I have nothing to lose except self-respect and honey, that went months ago.*

'You . . . you just talk as if there was nothing between us except this goddam exhibition,' she said dully.

'Well, you do want to do it, don't you?'

'You know fucking well that's not all I want to do. What the hell is going on, Lucy?'

'Perhaps I should go,' said Lucy. 'You're very angry with me.'

'Go!' said Jay, borrowing Baby Jane. 'Go! Just leave me alone again, why not, it's what you always do, just leave me alone with loving you, wanting you, needing you — why break the habits of a lifetime — GO!'

'Steady on,' said Lucy.

'I will not *steady on*,' said Jay. 'Why the fuck should I? Oh, it's OK for you, let's have an evening of work on the exhibition, your goddam son blew that out of the window once and I was supposed to say, 'Yes Lucy, no Lucy, three bags full, Lucy?' Hah! And now *you* want to work on the exhibition you were so all-fired about, I was so inspired by, same deal, huh? It's not the same deal.'

'God, you are angry,' said Lucy.

'Oh, had you noticed?' slashed Jay. 'Thank you so much. Recognition at last! Do not let me discommode you none, Miz Scarlett, I'm sure! Sorry, you're going.'

'No,' said Lucy, 'I haven't been fair to you. Let's try and sort this out.'

'Lend a hand and play the game?' Jay screamed. 'You make me sick. *Now* you want to be reasonable. Why? Make yourself feel better. Well, I don't feel better, Lucy. Fuck you!'

Which didn't phase Lucy. Which mode would she switch into next? Understanding parent of semi-alcoholic genius protégé? Surviving ex-wife or unreasonable alcoholic? Unwilling object of lesbian desire? Jay's brows fixed into furious question marks.

'I deserved that,' said Lucy, looking pale and tired behind the sun-gold glow (beat yourself up, Jay, you've hurt the one you love), 'but I said it wouldn't work. I said that weeks ago.'

'You said,' said Jay, *real B-movie melodrama here, kid!*, 'you said I'd have to decide for both of us. You said you couldn't handle it, but you didn't stick with that. I said we needed a weekend, real time, for both of us, and you said give it time. How much bloody time do you want?'

'Jay, it's not going to work. It's not a question of time.'

'Change your tune, why don't you!' said Jay. 'You call all the bloody shots round here!'

Lucy flung herself forward, cheeks flushed, eyes flashing. An emotional response! A hollow Hurrah! (As Jamie would say, compering a truly dreadful act.) It takes fury to rouse her?

'Christ!' she exploded, 'all this bloody drama over a few kisses!'

'Oh, fine,' said Jay on the unstoppable switchback of Nightmare Alley. 'Thank you! Now we're getting to it! My bloody heart and soul on the line and to you it's a 'few kisses' — you lousy hypocrite! I'm sorry. I failed to

realise that you kiss so easily. My mistake. Under-
standable, I think, after the huge deal you made over
even that. Fine! Fine! Relegate those few kisses to
ridicule, why don't you! Pardon me for thinking they
were important, pardon me for feeling beautiful and
lyrical, pardon me for loving you. I'll just fuck off and
forget it. Time is a great healer.'

'I didn't mean that,' said Lucy. 'You've been lovely to
me. It was very important to me, having you there,
caring for me. I'm very fond of you, Jay.'

Fond, in Jay's book, was what you were of plants,
distant and cute nieces and nephews, fond was a rice-
pudding emotion: it feeds, but never satisfies. Fond you
grow fat and sleepy with, fond and foolish: a grand-
motherly emotion, bric-à-brac, aspidistras and anti-
macassars. She was repulsed by the dark brown
chintzy respectability of fond: as well veil the piano legs
and wear a corset!

'Well, I'm not *fond* of you,' she drawled. 'I adore you,
your body drives me wild with desire, I live for the light
in your eyes, my whole being lights up at the thought of
you. And you know that. Jesus! I've written you poems
better than I ever dreamed I could write . . .'

'And I love your poems!' said Lucy, 'they're wonderful.
But Jay, that isn't me.'

'Who the hell else is it, excuse my amnesia,' said Jay. 'I
don't recollect writing poems for anyone else for
twenty years.'

'You're impossible!' said Lucy. 'I'm not who you think
— I'm not perfect. I'm someone you could do wonderful
world-changing things with. Your spark and my
organisation . . . and I'm a friend.'

'Friend?' said Jay, wearily. 'Friend? Lady, I want to
your lover.'

'CHRIST!' said Lucy hurtling to her feet, stalking the
floor like Mildred Pierce, 'all your talent and you just

want to be a bloody lover! You could really do something with your life, and *that's* what you want!'

'Yeah,' said Jay, 'and what's wrong with being a lover? You have some objection to appreciating your body, Lucy? You really think I can do this fucking exhibition, work on all these projects, sit beside you and keep my filthy lesbian hands to myself?'

Lucy paced, rampaged, flung out scads of unrequited ire, impassioned as Jay had never seen her.

'I'm fed up, sick, sick, sick to here with people saying I should be some other way! All of you! If only I was this, if I'd only said that, done the other — why always ME? Why can't you all just leave me be?'

'I don't know about anyone else,' said Jay, in the eerily calm eye of the storm, 'but you seemed to want me, seemed to be holding back from me and I don't know why. You wanted me sexually, goddammit, Lucy. I was THERE, and suddenly, you've decided no. And I want you so. I'm doing all this the wrong way, *I* know. Jesus, all I ever wanted was to love you, you to love me.'

Lucy flung herself full length on the floor, curled up and wept. Curled tight like an embryo that doesn't want to be born, like a baby who's had too much pain. Her weeping tore at her slender shoulders, white linen crumpling to folds of despair.

What do I do now, thought Jay, we've re-run *Who's Afraid of Virginia Woolf*, and what do I do now? Her body took over, she crossed to Lucy, lay beside her, curling round her, holding her close and Lucy turned, wept into her arms and Jay rocked and sh-sh-ed her, her flights of vituperation spent in the face of this pain. Suddenly Lucy unballed her fists from her face and kissed her, open mouthed, hard. Jay shushed her against her shoulder. What the hell was that kiss about in the middle of all this? Lucy wept. Lucy wept.

Jay was weirdly at peace. *You'll have to . . .*

'Come on,' she whispered, 'let's go to bed. You don't even have to take your fucking clothes off, darling, I want to hold all the hurt away. Let's go and lie on my bed, it's a hell of a sight more comfortable, let's just hold each other.'

Lucy said yes and Jay led her through to the other room. They lay and held each other. Lucy's sobs stilled a little and she clung to Jay. Kissed her. Jay covered her eyes and brow and cheek with kisses, Lucy's hand shook along her cheek.

'Take your clothes off and get into bed,' said Jay, a wave of calm sweeping over her. 'We don't have to do a thing you don't want. But I know what I want. I think I know what you want. Take your clothes off and let's see.'

'I have to pee,' said Lucy, all at once a child to be coaxed into the treat she wants.

'I'll follow you,' said Jay.

And returned to find Lucy in bed, duvet around her neck. She ripped her clothes to the floor.

'Come here, let me hold you,' said Jay.

She felt Lucy's heat-soft breasts nudge hers. Felt Lucy's slender arms round her shoulders. Felt her naked legs against Lucy's. She felt like every adagio ever written.

'Well, here I am in bed with a woman,' said Lucy. 'I've never done this before. I might just throw a total number. What am I doing, Jesus Christ, what am I doing?'

'The woman is me and I love you,' said Jay. 'Just hold tight, Lucy, Lucy, I love you.'

She kissed Lucy's brow, her eyebrows, her ears, her neck, her parted lips. Their tongues entangled. Her hand found Lucy's breast, her thumb found Lucy's nipple, Lucy drew closer as she stroked her belly, and her little finger exploded on the springy turf of Lucy's hair. So much she wanted to fling back the covers, light incense and candles, worship this adored body. But Lucy gripped her shoulders and Jay explored, dizzy with longing. How to tell, how to be the perfect lover, eight over the eight and exploding with tenderness.

Jay's hand played a sonata she'd never seen the score for. Lucy gasped and moved her hand on Jay's shoulders, kissed her with fire, thrust her whole body so close, head to toe. Jay's mind blew. Lucy was used to men, right? What to do, oh, what to do . . . her longing fingers moved deep inside Lucy, right to the hard bud of flesh, the flowing cervix.

'Jay, what are you *doing*?' murmured Lucy, the words broken by hauling breaths inside her.

'I'm loving you,' said Jay to Lucy's breast, 'Is it OK?'

'Mm,' said Lucy, writhing against her.

Jay rode that secret muscle for a while, her ears scanning every sigh. Her hand spiralled against Lucy's clitoris, goddamn the useless WORD for the centre of desire. Gentle and insistent, tender and rhythmic until Lucy came.

For Jay that was only a start.

'Zzthat OK for you?' she murmured.

'Yes,' said Lucy.

Jay coaxed around her desire.

'Zzthat really OK for you?' she said, her mouth yearning for more.

'You know it was,' said Lucy, abruptly, then as if making conversation. 'How about you?'

While she burned to have Lucy make love to her, that sudden in control precision made her say:

'I'm fine, fine.'

Time enough later for Lucy to know the sheer delight of making love to her.

And then Lucy had to go. Jay knew it, numbed herself against what it might mean.

Lucy wanted coffee, and Jay said sure, but keep your clothes off, took it back when Lucy said fine, no coffee. Came back to bed to find Lucy dressed in bed.

'But I've kept my bra off,' said Lucy.

They drank coffee, Jay's brain slurring off some awful truth. She held Lucy's breast. Lucy kissed her. Lucy went. She slept.

And woke in the morning knowing it, whatever it was, was over. You do not leave a new lover in the middle of the night. Something was appeased, and something had died. Very neatly and no one could say when, but something had died that night.

She dragged on a cigarette and wrote, as if words could change a thing.

CHAPTER TWENTY-SIX

the day after

feeling complete, replete, like a cat sleeping in the sun has all four paws buried under its furred belly, sun too hot to move, tail wrapped over its sleeping nose, I went back to our bed to curl up next to where you had been. Hadn't shifted one crease from the pillows where you sat and smoked and drank coffee, my hand on your warm naked breast. I lay as if you were there and loved the shape your back had made, had a sense of your silky warmth, my body curling round the heat and wonder of you in my arms.

One of your down-fine hairs was on the pillow: I picked it up like gold-dust – sweet relic! Another – I knelt delighted and collected your beautiful hair. Fox red, moonbeam silver, I held the precious strands like a pilgrim sips water from a miraculous spring.

I tiptoed to find a sacred vessel to keep your hair in, mouth humming with its knowing: you were here, with me, loving me, kissing me, holding me and could be no closer.

Sanctified by your presence, immortal in your beauty, your fire, loving you even more, when I loved you totally before.

And wishing, with a sunrise burst of longing to be with you always, to always be gentle as your hair is soft. So you would know . . . you know.

Oh, wild creature, it's you I've dared to demand in the garden of paradise. Wire-fragile, wind-trembling hare-bell. You are powerful like all creatures, fine-skinned and muscled to the bone, ears alert to every bracken rustle, the cries of the wheeling kites; the wind thrills you with its chill messages of danger and delight.

CHAPTER TWENTY-SEVEN

'So how's Lucy?' said Dionne over dinner, sparkling with anticipation. 'Did you pounce?'

'Yeah,' said Jay, 'I pounced.'

'And? Did she . . . oh, come on, puss, TELL me!'

'Well, it was very strange,' said Jay. 'We — did it —'

'She gave in! Wow! I never thought she would! Well done!'

Jay had to smile. True, she'd done it. Yes oh yes, she'd got Lucy in bed, made love — had sex? — fucked with? — there wasn't really a phrase to fit how utterly strange the whole thing had made her feel. An eerie shiver as she woke the next morning, suddenly in a cold landscape for which she had no bearings. There had been less between her and Lucy after the 'act' than ever before. It had been an end, where Jay had yearned to be sure — had been sure? what a fool believes? — it would be a beginning.

'So when are you seeing her?'

'Well, it's not quite like that. Hell, Dionne, it was so weird. I mean, we had this goddawful evening. She wouldn't have supper for a start. Like, it was work not socialising. But I thought, fuck, NOW you want to work? So we did this whole fury number: I was pissed as a fart, thankyou, Jamie, and I just threw the lot at her. Then she got really mad and started screaming back at me. It was George and Martha OK. Not OK.'

'Some people have to get wildly angry before they let themselves feel anything.'

'I dunno, dunno. Anyway, then she just sprawled on the floor and cried her heart out. I mean, weeping.'

'She's a strange one.'

'Mm. Anyway, I just held her, and it felt like she'd broken, couldn't take any more, then she kissed me. You know, sort of a sexual kiss, only really hard? So we went to bed.'

'Was it OK? I would assume with you it would be.'

'Thank you, precious. Well, it was. I mean, she seemed to be having a good time. I do aim to please. Only she said something as she was leaving — '

'She *left*?'

'Yeah. I said something like, well, I was trying to make her feel at ease, oh, something like, we could make a habit of this, and just have fun, Lucy. And she sort of sniffed and said, really shaky, *fun? that would be nice*. Like it was a foreign language.'

'Stupid woman,' said Dionne, but not unkindly. 'She can't let herself have fun?'

'Either that or she just doesn't fancy me, even *I* admit that possibility.'

'I don't think that's true. Having met her just that once, she was so sparky and ritzy. She couldn't look at you how she did and . . .'

'Dionne, very nice and all. I have always relied on the kindness of my friends. But I just felt *that's it*. Odd how I pinned so much on getting her into bed, and when I did, after we did . . . I just knew it was over.'

'Maybe you just need to give her time.'

'Not that one! If ever I meet a woman who says "give me time" again, I shall become a Carmelite!'

'Sorry, Jay. So what next? You seem dazed.'

'I feel numb. Last week at work — she always seems to have someone there when I am. Am I paranoid? Possibly — she just let drop that they're moving offices.'

'When?'

'Yesterday. She's gone. They've gone. Apparently they're expanding. She's promoted. Hertfordshire.'

'You should call her at home, Jay.'

'I did. She's gone ex-directory.'

'Christ,' said Dionne, 'Christ. Poor you. That's too much of a coincidence.'

'I tell myself she's got my number — in more ways than one. But she won't call. I even spent every evening last week in, in case. It's a dead one. Get some more wine, Dionne, this bottle hasn't touched me.'

'Baby, I don't know what to say,' said Dionne. 'Baby, get drunk and come and stay with me. You shouldn't be on your own.'

'I am on my own,' said Jay. 'And thanks, but I think I'd just bawl my eyes out all over you. Don't want to. I actually do believe baby requires a little time on her own.'

Numb, that was the feeling. Or lack of it. Floating in icy seas. And suddenly a sharp pain as if stabbed in the gut. A monstrous pain crackling along the frozen nerves to leave her dry crying, wordless sobs of abandonment. And when the words came through, pain stabbing through her brain and whipping round her body like barbed wire, words digging into the flesh.

It took more and more gin and wine to shut the words up, pick out the barbs.

Catatonic.

Dully punching Lucy's old number, slamming the phone down on *unattainable*.

Had it been that bad?

Was she that lousy a lover?

If only it was that simple.

I think, said Jay aloud to herself, I do believe I'm going mad.

Then so be it.

CHAPTER TWENTY-EIGHT

Jay at three in the morning — *hello, young lovers, wherever you are!* — drunk, suddenly *had* to see a picture of Lucy. But the contact sheet she'd taken from the office was not in her bag, not in any of the half dozen dead newspapers lying round the floor, not under any of the piles of flung-down clothes, not under the sofa, not in the bin. When you're drunk you check everything eight times, lurching like a pain-maddened rhinoceros. Surely she hadn't chucked it out?

Sure enough Jay at ten past three in the morning flits down the stairs of the crumbling house in her pomegranate kimono, mad woman in search of photo, as if a photo could help her understand. Becomes Ms. Melancholy Moonwailer, is anybody there? On the doorstep of the night-time house, imagining herself locked out by a freak wind slamming the door shut. It doesn't. She isn't. The street is moondark and utterly without sound, the city a smoky neon backdrop. She lugs the most recent bag of trash back up the stairs, unties it, putrid stench, fermenting and ghastly like old fruit skins. Jay gags, this is where love has brought me, rooting through the bins like a vagrant, looking for a sheet of high-gloss photographic paper and a bad profile shot of Lucy smaller than a postage stamp.

Oh, well. I've lost it, thought Jay. Congratulations, bitch, what else is new? Thought you were so damn smart getting it in the first place, and drink has blurred you so much you've blown it.

Back to bed. On the radio, Peter from Crawley whittering some sort of shit, what? Bisexuals are animals, aren't they, Brian? just bloody animals. Ring Brian again and again for the relief of talking to someone in this Lucyless silent world, engaged, engaged, engaged.

Then her rolling eye caught the edge of the contact sheet — by her bed all the time. Squinted at the dark shot: Lucy smiling, glass and cigarette balanced, somebody talking right to her, Lucy charming, Lucy,

Jay rang the Samaritans.

She had always thought she was not the type to ring the Samaritans.

But before falling in love with Lucy, she was not the type to lie awake, miss meals, weep, miss work, lose weight, have eczema, fall asleep with the light and fire blazing, feel hopeless, feel that everything was more or less meaningless, be unable to cope.

All this love had brought her, taught her: the flip side of ecstasy. Boy, thought Jay, am I ever paying my dues.

'It's not like you to be ill,' her mother said. Well, wrong again.

Cry me a river? Cry me Niagara, not crying wolf this time: yup, thought Jay tossing Lucy's photo away, away out of sight but never mind, I am Ms. Melancholy Moonwailer, whingeing on to a total stranger at four in the morning.

'Samaritans. Can I help you?'

Mummy mummy.

'I'm not suicidal or anything,' said Jay. 'I just can't sleep.'

CHAPTER TWENTY-NINE

It was the in-between of that sludge-grey spring that stopped and started, flowers bursting out then drenched with sleet, blighted by snow; skies grey and thundery, rain mean and seeping, wind a slinking greasy cur that has paddled through filthy city ponds and has nowhere to go.

And Jay was pacing her attic, bars tightening and cracking around a heart that would not stop hurting; she could not lay her body down though it screamed for rest and knots of fury made her neck and shoulders a steely hunch like a vulture. Her face in the mirror looked raddled, eyes wild and angry and pained, mouth set. She felt every one of her thirty some years sitting on her face, and stared at this disoriented stranger, her self. You make your face.

I do not understand!

She fretted against the invisible glass, the cool and unbridged chasm between Lucy and herself, paced the crumbling edge. So short a time ago they had found and shared a grassy path in a brief Eden of summer-blue skies, tapestry green and flowered meadows, every day a delight, the world a beautiful old master cleaned in the zephyr of Lucy's being.

And now.

London had been grit grey for months, and Jay fought the sunless skies with the blade of keen memory. It was not even as noble and hopeless as tilting at windmills; she was blindfolded by not understanding and whirled towards every sound — Lucy's voice, laugh, profile, light footfall: all worn by unknowing everyday strangers. She was challenging the shadows of shadows, challenging the shadows of primeval monsters half-glimpsed in nightmare.

I am alone on a desolate plain, and I am cold and I am lonely thought Jay, chanted Jay, she could find no comfort. Finally, she had rung the new office, cursing herself, her need. Lucy would not see her.

I feel I have unfinished business with you said Jay, amazed that she could use such an adult phrase, when alone, her mouth sagged and stretched and gasped with *momma, momma*, the pain shrieked from her navel, she even sucked her thumb in the hope that do-it-yourself primal therapy would ease something. It did not.

Yes, I expect you do, said Lucy, a tiny precise voice in her ear, *but I am not the one to help you.*

Politeness, adulthood, monsters, nonsense. Jay demanded, her voice ugly, feeling so far away she could lose no more, the angrier she grew the further Lucy went; but when she forced herself to be quiet and good, Lucy still kept her distance.

FUCK YOU! screamed Jay. It wasn't what she meant. She slammed the phone down, shook and smoked. Then firmed her jaw and imagined the tight lines she was seeding round her mouth. I shall be a bitter-looking little old lady with no muscle tone, she thought, and re-dialled Lucy.

I'm sorry, she lied, beside herself, *but I need to talk to you.*

Come over later and have a cup of tea, said Lucy, each word measured, sounded cold and reasonable, just a cup of tea in front of the fire and no heavies from either of us. OK?

What's made you change your mind? said Jay ungraciously, *I won't take hand-outs from you!*

I've looked at my diary, said Lucy. OK?

OK, said Jay, I'm sorry. I'm so sorry.

Alone again, and knowing that a cup of tea was what was offered only after screaming and shouting and throwing all her nice toys on the floor. She felt like a bad child, a bad little girl who wouldn't give up. And what was that sorry about? Sorrow itself.

> *my pain is that I knew you*
> *and you will only have me as a stranger*
> *a dangerous acquaintance*
> *an episode you apologise for*
> *my sorrow is that we will never kiss again*

And so to tea. Jay swore she would behave herself, awkward in Lucy's tidy living room, her table between them had a map of the world on it. Jay half smiled. Once more together. Worlds apart.

Good God! She couldn't look at Lucy's face. Hopeless laughter curled around her hollowness. All this drama, darling, she thought all this gotta-see-her, and I can't even look at her. She sneaked a glance while Lucy poured tea. Then studied the ceiling as the tears would not be checked. That, my dear, she said, is why you can't look at her. And I do not give you permission to fling yourself at her feet, grab her hands and weep into her palms.

So well-behaved was Jay that Lucy relaxed. Jay couldn't remember why it had been so important to see her. The person across the room was Lucy, Lucy without love. No longer so important.

So relaxed was Lucy that she offered Jay wine.

I guess I had to see you, drawled Jay, *because I was so scared of seeing you. I don't want to be scared of anything.*

You see, said Lucy, I was never in love with you. I'm very fond of you.

Jay looked at the ceiling. *I was never in love with you.* She'd said it. She'd robbed those stolen kisses of their delight, and if not ever in love, then why, what the hell had she meant? How can her eyes and hands and breasts meet and mingle and Lucy say categorically, like not for one minute or second or fleeting flit of time, never never never had she been in love. Chin up, Jay, she told herself, you needed to hear that. You have to let go or go mad.

She let the silence go on, and wondered about just getting up and leaving right then without one word, not one word of the torrent foaming in her guts.

I was never in love with you.

CHAPTER THIRTY

She was coming to the end of months on the barren atoll of Pity Me when she heard the moth rattle against her window, between tacked-up scarlet and black batik fabric and the glass. Jay had a horror of moths flying into her face and hair; she liked to think of herself as someone who cups her hands for moths and spiders and frees them. But she didn't. She jumped round the room with a newspaper club and splattered them when they settled. She washed spiders down the plughole, and felt guilty as hell about it. Imagined hairy great mutant legs straining against the plug and prying it upwards.

So, the moth. It was late one night running into horribly early the next morning. Jay had picked up a pattern of sleeplessness over the last five months. Her sleeve of care was unravelled all right: her life was a basket of woollen shreds, all shades and textures and not one of them long enough to do anything with. As if she'd been wearing a coat of many many colours, and, beached on the desert island shore of Pity Me, had shredded the damn shrunken thing. Without it she was cold, but simply hadn't the energy or inclination to weave it into anything new and warm. Tides and tears had faded and roughened every strand.

Her bedroom had become a nest. A crow's nest high above the street, a magpie's nest, phone light fire scads of books juice vitamin pills cold tea tobacco papers matches ashtray diary address book radio all within reach of the heap of pillows and quilts, tangled sheets and herself. Jay had taken up situationist sculpture, and eased herself half upright to look at yesterday evening's achievement. Ah yes! Corduroy Jeans On Upright Hoover — one of her best. Counterposing this stark image . . . Dead Boots Gawping With Limp Sock Tongues.

Gee, what a dump.

Sleep came, knocked her out some way past four. She woke with the radio and light on. The moth was still fluttering between the pane and pinned scarlet cotton.

RoboJay took over in the morning. Put the kettle on,

spooned coffee, rolled a cigarette, sat up in bed again and hoped the horrors had forgotten her address.

Jay liked to phone her friends in the morning. A sort of hi I'm here and how are you, have a nice day. She was actually giggling with Francis when the moth swooped into the cave: her light and ever-shaded windows guaranteed a sort of candlelit stalactite effect. Of course the moth went for the light, Jay went under the pillow, and the moth settled on a huge picture she had of a golden African dawn.

It was in fact a butterfly, tawny orange like a tiger with a purple and black lace frill to its wings. It shuttled around on the picture. She couldn't kill a butterfly. Even one daft enough to wake up in early February. She had a bath.

Her house was falling down, a tree growing out of the chimney, and purple buddleia all summer from the guttering and up over her windowsills. This fool butterfly must have been a chrysallis — there are a million tortoiseshells pirouetting on the purple flowers all the warm months — a chrysallis left from last August. Fooled by the fake spring amazing everyone into bright cotton, courtesy of a destroyed ozone layer and a rogue wind from the Sahara. Poor butterfly. There was sweet nothing in the way of nectar and what duped flowers had burst out of the ground were in for a shock when the frosts came.

'Hum,' Jay said to Francis over their café breakfast, 'I have a butterfly in my bedroom.'

'Oh,' said he. 'You'd better buy it some flowers. It must be starving.'

'They only live a day,' said a loony from the next table.

'That's mayflies,' Jay said. She left to do some shopping and forgot the flowers. Poor butterfly. It was nowhere in sight.

But the sun tugged her out of bed the next day and

there was the butterfly, still fluttering. Jay unpinned the batik, unscrewed the lock and pushed the window up. Now all Madame Butterfly had to do was climb down a piece of wood twice her height and fly free. Bright little creature — it took her just three minutes to work this out as her antennae fluttered in the sudden sweet smelling breeze. Jay watched her go, dip down, dip up, over the edge of the guttering.

Two weeks later it snowed, Jay thought of the butterfly as the thick white flakes tumbled around. Hoped to God she had found a leaf somewhere. But in a moment, the sun was blazing, the sky blue as cornflowers.

CHAPTER THIRTY-ONE

Jay's life had not exactly prepared her for falling In Love, still less for *I was never in love with you.* How to make sense of Lucy and this dizzying all-consuming pain; how to find a meaning for her life which had only acquired meaning with Lucy as its radiant centre. Not just an incomprehensible episode, but a meaningless present.

So she ran through those utterly devastating transformations when she had been In Love, desperately seeking patterns, pointers — digging for something to bring back her joy, her *I will survive.*

First time she was seventeen. And now, nearly twenty years after it was well and truly over, she sometimes still reeled late at night with not understanding. *Baby where did our love go, what went wrong, what did I do wrong?*

Francis just made a tragi-comic face and said:

'Darling, I don't even understand ME! No one ever understands anyone, dear. I don't know why you bother. Give it up!'

And why did she bother? How could she and how could she not give it up? Because it drove her every moment. Her skin was alive with the memory of Lucy's touch; her fingertips alive with Lucy's skin; her lips an agony and ecstasy of kissing Lucy. She read that your life's work is finding who you are and then being it. At thirty-seven she could only say for sure who she was not and she felt that time was running out.

Would it have been easier if she hadn't seen Lucy almost every day for four years going into or out of the office next door? Seeing her had become part of her life, first pleasant, then ecstatic, then the whole reason for being. The corridor held memories, the walls recalled shadows, the floor echoed with the sound of her walk. The ecology people were still mailing all sorts of publications to her, and her mouth would set hard with pain when she read Lucy's name in a list of credits or committee members.

But she was gone. For Jay absence had only ever made the heart grow fonder. Now, absence paralysed her in sheer aching agony. Jesus, she raged, my life is a string of clichés.

'OK,' said Francis, 'I've given you months, darling. Slenderness is one thing, anorexia another; heart-broken agony is one thing, living pain is just not right. You need a holiday. The magazine will just have to lurch along snuggled up to me and my ageing haemorrhoids for a few weeks. Go away. Take care of yourself. Go.'

In fact Francis booked the holiday and drove her to the airport.

'Get drunk,' he advised. 'I would recommend a little holiday romance.'

'I don't give myself permission, Francis,' said Jay. 'Imagine inflicting myself on anyone in this state. I'd burst into tears all the time. I've just had open-heart surgery, remember?'

'You must just forget, dear. Scrub round it. Lucy is bad for your psyche. And it's a very nice psyche.'

CHAPTER THIRTY-TWO

Jay sat on the white balcony, shaded from a Mediterranean sun burning off white walls, sparking off a turquoise sea where the bright sails of a skiff were silk balloons shot with dazzle, sparkles of pure light bursting behind the boat as it skimmed the perfect waters.

She had brought detective novels and thrillers and cursed her hectic reading speed: only the second day and she was half-way down the pile. But then she shrugged: every plot was so eminently forgettable, she could start again, once she was through.

She watched her bare toe rub against the whitened concrete of the balcony. It was a nice toe, she decided. Here's to you, toe, she said, raising her long clear glass of white wine and mineral water, where the ice cubes had long since melted. That's what holidays were for — looking at your toes, wandering on the beach, hours of sitting and staring, standing and staring, lying as long as you could bear in the sun with eyes closed. The perfect place to mend a broken heart — no, she said, stop that — a *jaded* heart and soul.

And a certain party's name was not to cross her mind, rather, if it did, she was to wipe it out with a picture of her favourite places, backed by her favourite music. So far she'd run a mind-movie of Malvern with Elgar, the Outer Hebrides with Mendelssohn, Box Hill with Vivaldi, Santa Cruz with The Beach Boys, Baltimore with Laurie Anderson, and Corfu with Grieg. Well, it was only her second day.

The night before she had woken uneasy. Was it the sound of someone crying close at hand? But the dark night was filled with the metallic throbbing of insects, waves on the sand, and she got up and stood naked on the balcony. The moon was a slender crescent, and a few tattered clouds shuffled across the perfect dome of blue-black sky. She watched as night-grey filtered out to recognisable shapes: the beached boats, the shifting edge of the sea, the low houses slung along the road.

There was a light in the next window and she drew back into deep shadow. The off-season hotel had been empty when she arrived. They were expecting Club 18-30, but she would be long gone before that intrusion. Company she did not want.

You will find us very quiet, the manager had said, c'est la vie.

They were eight merciful miles from a holiday mecca. Over on the horizon there was a dark-blue smudge of land to be seen only in first clear light. The hotelier said it was Italy. The ceiling of the Sistine Chapel. Uh oh.

She stretched and showered, screamed along with a flashback of Jamie at The Pink Flamingo and *There ain't nothin' like a dame!* She sauntered back to the view and Miss Blandish, but swept her sunglasses on with instinctive irritation as she saw a figure on the next balcony. She held a book as if reading and sipped wine.

Five yards away a woman sat almost in profile, a white towelling robe easy on her shoulders. She held a book, reached out to a tall glass of pale gold wine, a twin to Jay's. She bent and fiddled with a machine at her feet.

God! thought Jay, stiffening, bloody radios!

But she relaxed at the sound of Schubert. The sure delicacy of the notes tripped through the air, dancing in the glare of the sun, moving with the light breeze in the parched trees, the uneasy rustle in the blue-green dune grass. Jay smiled. If there must be a neighbour, let her have good taste. And foresight enough to bring her own music.

The woman had short very black hair, stylishly cut away from the curve of her jaw; her head was upright, and her firm chin rested on one hand. A tendril of smoke lazed through the air from a cigarette. Her skin was pale, and as Jay watched, she leaned forward and massaged sun-cream into her calves with such concentration and pleasure that Jay was transfixed.

Suddenly the woman turned.

'Oh, I'm sorry,' she called, when she saw Jay. '*Mille pardons!*'

She switched off the music.

'No, no,' said Jay, 'it's OK. Please. I love Schubert. Really.'

'Really?' said the woman anxiously. Jay realised her dark glasses cut off eye contact. She took them off.

'Yes,' she said, 'I'd love you to play more. Here's to Schubert!'

She raised her glass, smiled briefly as the woman raised hers, and looked down at her book.

The music continued, and the print flowed past Jay's eyes. At the third corpse there was a faint click, and she looked up as the music stopped. The woman had gone inside.

Shame, thought Jay, that was very pleasant.

You can tell we're English, she thought that evening as they sat four tables apart in the dining room, books propped against their separate water jugs. The waiter flurried between them, as busy as if the room were full. A huge local family came in as she was drinking coffee, and suddenly there were voices and laughter as they arranged the stately grandmother at the head of the table, the boisterous children banished to the other end. On an impulse, Jay scribbled a note and beckoned the waiter.

The woman turned a page of her book.

'*Un Armagnac pour la dame – là – s'il vous plait,*' said Jay.

'*L'anglaise?*' said the waiter, impassive.

'*Oui,*' she said, and gave him the folded note.

The woman looked up as the waiter made a great show of placing the glass with its golden contents beside her, and nodded his head towards Jay. The woman turned and looked frankly puzzled, unfolding the note. Then she smiled, radiant, but God, she looked weary. The note has said simply: *Merci pour Schubert.* She raised her glass to Jay, then gathered bag and book and paused at Jay's table.

'I'm glad you like Schubert,' she said.

'Yes,' said Jay, smiling. 'You do like Armagnac, I hope?'

'Oh, yes,' said the woman, 'thank you.'

'Do join me,' said Jay, 'if you like.'

'Perhaps we could have a drink outside,' said the woman as the French family exploded with bellowed laughter and banging fists.

'*Deux Armagnacs, s'il vous plaît*' said Jay to the waiter and they strolled to the table outside the hotel. They sat at the edge of the patio where vines trailed a dusky scent.

'I admire your foresight,' said Jay. 'I always forget to bring music.'

'I couldn't be without it,' said the woman. 'Do you like Mozart?'

'Oh, yes,' said Jay.

'I shall play some tomorrow,' said the woman, sipping brandy.

The light from the window spilled along her cheek and lips, and made a dazzling star in her glass. Jay smiled from her shadow, admitting a lazy, faint and wholly delicious curl of desire.

'Mozart can be anywhere,' she said, 'one of the immortals.'

'Everywhere,' said the woman intensely. 'And to think he was thirty-three when he died.'

'Like Christ,' said Jay.

The sea soughed on the shore. They drank another Armagnac.

Jay had no inclination to go through the who are you, what do you do, oh really, gosh my brother-in-law used to be in the same field. And the woman showed no signs of starting either. There was something about the firm set of her body that Jay knew instinctively: she was a survivor. Another survivor. She and her music would get through it; just as Jay was forcing herself to thrive on an inimitable diet of white wine and forties Chicago gangland trash.

Suddenly, it was chill.

'I think I'll go to bed,' said Jay.

'I'll have a stroll,' said the woman, 'haven't taken any exercise all day.'

'*A demain*,' said Jay. It would be nice to see her tomorrow.

'Sweet dreams,' said the woman.

She was too far away to speak before Jay realised they hadn't even exchanged names.

She strolled upstairs. The air was incredibly hot, and she opened the balcony doors. Caught sight of her neighbour's small grey shape against the blanched sand. She poured herself more brandy and sat on the balcony, invisible against the dark room.

The woman was wandering at random, in loose zig-zags it seemed, until Jay's eyes picked out the curling shifting edge of the sea. She was skirting the moving foam, a foot away, and jumped sideways when a wave overreached. After a while, Jay could no longer pick her out against the distant sand, and she lay on the bed, under a sheet, downed the last of her drink, and slept.

At three she woke with an uneasy feeling. Someone was crying, from the guts of misery. Jay located the sound: it was the woman next door.

But she couldn't fit that self-contained assurance and elegance with this lost and hopeless sobbing. Should she knock? She wanted to: Jay could not bear people suffering. But if she was wrong? She sensed through the darkness, brow creased. The crying stopped, and she breathed easier. She went on to the balcony, pulling on her silk kimono against the cold night.

'Oh, hello,' said the woman on the next balcony. 'Couldn't sleep?'

It was a voice which takes charge, organises and copes.

'No,' said Jay. 'You?'

'Must be the sea air,' said the woman briskly. 'Can't get a wink.'

'Coffee?' said Jay, wondering at herself.

'No, thank you,' said the woman. 'I'd never sleep. But thanks.'

Fine, thought Jay, wincing at the way she always overstepped the mark. You're a fucking crusader! had been yelled at her more than once.

She lay in bed. Ouch. Now, what about a walk down the River Shannon with a merry fiddle and a melancholy flute? She fell asleep dreaming dragonflies. She rose early, determined to walk the day away, give the woman her space. They had both clearly come here to be alone. Let it be so, she decided, as she went into the empty dining room.

CHAPTER THIRTY-THREE

A mile or so along the sand, she sat on a rock, looking at the grey/indigo streak of Italian coastline. The sun coaxed her body to stretch idly as a cat; she tanned easily, adored white heat and turquoise sea. Always wondered what brought her back to the miseries of soggy grey England, the endless winters.

Oh, dear. Here comes that name again. Right. Corfu. Corfu the first time, years ago, the summer of Laurie Anderson and *O Superman*; the summer she was in love with a difference. The summer she was loved back.

Two weeks on perfect sand in sunshine nine to five; she'd returned with an all-over tan feeling wonderful and hey presto, head over heels in love with Astrid! And she was Astrid's first woman. Astrid was married, kids and mortgage, but the summer had rocketed by in a riot of colours and joy, and autumn found Astrid divorced and coming to the end of being in love with Jay.

Some you win, thought Jay, however briefly. She remembered their passion for Louis Prima, Fats Waller, Chris Williamson; wild about holographic badges, earrings, stickers.

Turquoise glass beads from Murano against Astrid's tanned arm; she wore pastel turquoise dungarees, a tee-shirt the deep green blue of southern seas in a late afternoon. That's why Jay thought her eyes were blue.

She told her how beautiful they were, how there had never been such a blue.

I have one thing to say to you, said Astrid laughing, two weeks apart and letters every day later, *my eyes are green!*

Green eyes.

Her eyes were also grey like stones through clear water.

Pre-Astrid, Jay had been in a dead job, art workshops with utterly disillusioned teenagers, every morning she coughed she rang in sick, malingering Mondays, rain seeped in the doors of the empty bus every morning, the bus to the High Street for the next bus, hoping to be early enough to miss the screaming leering sneering schoolgirls she had to face all day. She was a washed-out wash-out, *Miss, why're you such a div?*

After she fell in love with Astrid, she became Dragon-fly Moonchild, the world her oyster, and for the first time on the daily journey, she saw an adventure playground over the hoardings by the Elephant and Castle, and all the poles were painted like a carousel. Suddenly, there were trees and they were spring-green. She dragged herself from the smoke and choke and bitch and groan of the staffroom every lunchtime to sit in the rose garden in the park. No children or dogs to spoil the gold-fished lily pond. Old people in lavender and tweed sitting against the neat hedges, and roses tumbling along veined and curled beams, timber dry-docked after a lifetime at sea.

That week, exam week, all she had to do was invigilate. She wrote letters all day, floated around on a lilac cloud, heart beating scarlet with desire for Astrid and the tingling delight of waiting for when she would return. From the family holiday in Tunisia, to come and stay with Jay — no question that they would be lovers! Jay's rainbow wings fluttered around a sun-sparkling river that had become her life, where she had been moping by an old canal full of dead shopping trolleys for years.

They had a summer full of sand and sea and gold, Jay was blessed with that summer and the sunshine of Astrid's love. But she, she shed her loves in autumn like the trees, and Jay was gusted away in the chill, too late to chrysallis, too late to fly south, too late. And that was the end of Dragonfly Moonchild.

For years afterwards, Jay's heart gave a lurch every time she passed the place where they parked — Astrid drove the three hundred yards from her house so they could kiss in the car before she went to Tunisia.

They made love in Jay's co-op basement and wandered in Brick Lane market. They giggled with bagels in a park strewn with dog-shit and broken bottles, and pretended it was New York.

They painted Astrid's house and made love all the time.

They flirted with everybody especially each other.

Only last summer, years after it was all over and Astrid had found her stone cottage with roses round the door, golden/grey in a late summer orchard, she met Jay, and her eyes were green as the flames on ashwood.

Firelight, evening light.

Ho hum.

In love meant all the colours, all the sounds, all the sights, sheer joy. But out of love brought ice-age chill, endless snow wastes where wind tossed smoky columns of snow eighty foot high; from these mists lumbered a gallery of primitive animals, blood lust and need raging like her soul. Their hunger was hers, their battle-scarred pelts ached with the gashes on her heart. The voice, the vacuum of denial screamed from her navel, and oh the cold! After love, it was night in the desert, handfuls of icy sand stinging her skin and eyes. And then it was mammoth time and nothing she could do about it.

Yes, Dragonfly Moonchild she had been and loved the summer-child in her.

Jay shivered in the solid sunshine and forced memories of the winter after that summer. It had all crystallised at a party. She should not have gone to that party. She closed her eyes and played it back, as if from a great height. Crew-cut Jay, bristling with rage. Not a pretty sight.

CHAPTER THIRTY-FOUR

Once again, she was drunk.

That whole winter she drank with no pleasure. She and Astrid had lollopped through gin sparkling with fresh limes and tonic; late-night hand-warmed brandy, summer wines lighting each day. She drank automatically when It was over, noticed only when her glass was empty and didn't let it stay that way long.

Oh no, I'm drunk again. The comic voice and no one's laughing.

The first kiss of alcohol warms and soothes the snarling. They didn't want me at this party, but because I AM, fang and claw I have grapple-hooked their smooth cliffs, and have the right to stalk these wooded cliffs, lap at their abundant streams. And I do.

Skulk to the waterhole. One drink and the skulk howls away into the night, lean arrogance holds her upright, one shoulder against the wall. She bares her beautiful fangs and her rough pelt fluffs dry, sleek in the subtle Habitat lighting. Eyes glitter with a memory of the chill snowfields that once claimed her. Her civilised paw curves round a glass.

And they stare, can't stop, they know what is said of the claws, the biting words from her jaws, and a shiver tightens the pores of their hairless flesh. They have seen her in the shadows outside the windows of country cottages, and drawn the blinds, dropped the latch.

> *some mangy wolf*
> *its rough rust frame*
> *on brittle legs of blasted black*
>
> *– snarl of a husk of hedgerow*
> *ranging the dusk full field . . .*

She lounges through the party rooms, a scent of snow as she passes. The bevelled painted doorframe is a winter tree. A glow behind her shaggy head is moonlight, cloud scarred at the change of seasons. She stakes out her territory.

'Sit down, I'll get you a drink.'

Weary muscles and taut sinews soothed, she stretches on the carpet. The room arranges itself around her form. They come with a glass. Wariness in their eyes. Propitiation. The liquid brings blood to her face. The faces around her suppliant, wary — she is in a benevolent lull, she measures out wit and wisdom. They bring more drink.

Soon her tongue unleashes. Behind the words a memory of the pack. Where she learnt savagery. Where she would lie still, huddled close to fur scarred and torn, half dead with cold and hunger. Then jerk away, lope alone from the despised warm pulse of life. Born to the pack, but not of it. In her eyes the madness of a starvation that will be satiated, the tempered contempt of one who will survive. Alone.

'Oh no, she's off again.'

The group hears, leers, regroups away from the warning ripples from her slumped body. At her eye level, well-shod heels, well-heeled shoes, above, her, elegantly tailored backs. She attempts a snarl, lost in the chit-chat.

Someone sits beside her, a clutch of coals in the snow. Stay. Be warmed. Rest. Be petted. Stay. But she fears the embers' flicker and the night closing in over chill ash. The heels and backs and murmurs are darkness and call a howl from her cells; she lies, almost out of it. The embers die as she denies their warmth. A final flare in the icy wind, the hand is dashed away and lies helpless.

She rises, pushing at the carpet, the wall, the door-frame, unsteadily through the party. Lurch. Sorry. Bump. Sorry. Slop. Sorry. Sorry, sorrysorrysorry. Each sorry a slorry slurred whine. She is wearing her party smile which slashes to a snarling slaver and she makes it to the kitchen where cold steel lies on Dutch tiles. Claw and fang.

'Pissed again?'

She manoeuvres to face the voice. It repeats its mocking through the haze. The room is dazzling snow, the moon has risen full and cold. The night the pack turned on her, fury in their lean need. Scars throb, pain brings blood to her head and her great paws close on the knife.

'Who asked you, bastard?'

Rasped from her gashed throat. They left her, left her to drag herself bleeding to death . . . she did not die.

She pitches forward. The knife clatters on quarry tiles.

'Bloody lunatic!'

'The woman's an animal!'

'Oh, shit, do *I* have to take her home?'

'She's not staying here.'

They bundle the puppet-jointed body into the car. It slumps, jolts as it is driven. Street lamps streak her face, a voice streaks unconscious ears as the driver curses the dark, the hour, the traffic, the bloody liability sprawled on the back seat.

Three a.m. and the door knocks in the dark street.

'She's pissed again. God, she's done this once too often. This is . . . oh HELL!'

The body sags against the door, the heavy arms rest around necks and shoulders. They handle the massive limp débris.

Consciousness flickers. Tomorrow, sorry, sorry. Tomorrow bravado. She digs claws deep into their shoulders, arches her spine against them. Still they hold and help and she, she needs needs . . . needs to . . .

She flings her great head at one of them and rests against a skull. Breath drags in. A final effort.

Fighting the shadows in the dark air, she bares her teeth and sinks them deep, through hair, through pulsing flesh, to the bone.

That winter had been savage, she had been savage that winter. What had redeemed her? Oh, yes, she remembered, inwardly arching her eyebrows! *hmm, so you recall, do you, Jay?*

Surprise, surprise it had been:

Falling in love again.

With Dionne. Delight that she could be stirred by another person. They had flirted from the word go, had a lorra lorra fun, in bed and out. Dionne said it wasn't love, but who's counting? The sex had drifted away after a while, and Jay didn't mind; not in that end-of-the-world Astrid way. And Dionne stayed friends; a friend who fucked sometimes.

Jay had then sworn off love.

Too painful, darling!

And then came Lucy.

Jay had run out of travelogue and music. Well, not quite, but she felt safer after the memory of other loves, other times when she had been happy. And the beginning of Lucy and her had been lyrically beautiful, the stuff that dreams are made of. Live your dreams!

Forget the last six months, admit it's been more like a year, remove yourself from the desperate turns on the rack of rejection . . . at least you know how to love. Words bubbled in Jay's mind with an absurdly happy smile. She reached for her notebook and cigarettes and played the words around, wielded their texture and richness to sculpt a poem to her joy.

A poem for *her* eyes only, a poem she liked. There would be no more In Love redemption, thought Jay, in fact all she knew was that she didn't know what Love was. Some conclusion, Baby Jay!

She decided to treat herself as good as she would if she was In Love with Jay.

For example, now, she would be gathering shells to show to The Beloved, searching for ways to describe the perfect Disney sky. She felt like a total loony doing these things for herself. Perhaps that was why people who talked to themselves usually had an abstracted smile: they had accepted they were stark raving mad, loony tunes, round the twist. *We're all maaa–aaaaaaaad, darling!*

And walked back to the hotel minus her ball and chain.

As May Sarton had said (and Jay thought of May Sarton as a cross between a saint and a guru): *The muse is always female.*

Jay lived best when inspired; for her love had always

been the inspiration; she lived and wrote from passion, passion which led to the abyss. But always out of it again. Rose, Astrid, Dionne (a little), and now the chasm of Lucy. Could she do this one alone? Break a pattern and emerge into the daylight without the hovering angel face of a new *In Love*? Did she only feel good because of the unexpected fillip of her highly attractive anonymous new neighbour?

Certainly that was a part of it: fear of in love and rejection had sent Jay along the sands away from her, away from the pattern of I-love-her, she-loves-me-not. It wasn't even love.

I fancy her, said Jay aloud. I fancy her, and why the hell not?

Enjoy, enjoy! Jay stripped her clothes off and plunged into the sea, still smiling! Ha, you demons, she thought with every foam-headed wave cuffing her, there's a dance in the old dame yet! Floating beyond the foam, she closed her eyes against the sun.

The problem, she thought, in the hotel room, dressing to delight herself, delighted to be objective, to be smiling still, the problem: how to do all that, how to feel alive and brimming without a love object.

But, suddenly, spooning soup, a bitter bubble of self-loathing stopped Jay's throat. From deep inside, a jeer, a sneer.

'Yah! Look at you!' it spat. 'Who are you trying to kid?'

She froze her face. Tears again, she felt like the child she had been when her father gave wild stinging slaps to her legs by way of welcome after she'd run away from home. His was the snarling rage, hers the shame as she peed and peed and swore one day to be big enough to beat him, razor his skin, utterly humiliate him, and scorn his cries for mercy. The voice continued: she listened, telling it *Damn you! Speak your frowsty worst — go on!*

'Yeah,' it said with relish, 'you think you'll forget about your precious Lucy just because you're a few hundred miles away? Pathetic, that's what you are, futile. You never forget anything, you never let go. Jesus! If she crooked her precious little finger you'd be running. You'll be weeping about Lucy when you're fifty and fat.'

Go on, she told the voice with deadpan strength, *futile, fat, fifty, is that your worst?*

'You stink,' said the voice, steely cold. 'You never do anything right, you never do anything for the right reasons. You always fuck up.'

Useless to list her achievements under this acid rain of self-destruction.

'Gah!' said the filthy creature worming along her bones and veins, 'you thought you'd *chat up* that woman, didn't you?'

Maybe.

'Maybe?!' the voice raised a shaggy eyebrow. 'She looks a little like your Lucy, had you noticed? Your Lucy? Let's get the facts right. Not your Lucy, never was, never will be. Do you think you can fool me, Armagnac at sunset? Out of love and in again? Do you really believe love can save you from *you?*'

Jay could have slammed her head against the table and wept. The scourging voice always did this, whatever golden kernel of hope she treasured, so scared of losing it, it was almost a secret even to herself . . . the voice seized it, shredded it, pissed on it, trampled it. All the time with other people she was acting, confident and charming; backstage alone, the pain in her eyes glared at her from a bright-lit make-up mirror, weeping at the tawdriness of it all, scorning costume and plot and witty script.

'You don't fool me!' The voice surveyed the wasteland it had made and stormed away. Whimper like a whipped puppy, Jay, have a drink and pick up the pieces. Alcohol and phonecalls, after an attack she would not let herself be too sober or alone. Her dreams at these times were of running headlong down streets and staircases, into cellars where the roof and walls closed in on her. Running as the street collapsed behind her, running as if from Sodom and Gomorrah, from a nuclear blast. She never looked back to see what was chasing her, just woke in a cramped sweat, breathless and in tears.

CHAPTER THIRTY-FIVE

But she had read that if you turn and face the nameless fear, just once, you never have that dream again.

OK.

You're just an animal!

Jay decided to gamble with this thing inside her, deep as her blood and bones. Gambling to lose her demons. She had felt so free and lithe along the beach. The stakes were high.

Let's play, then, she said, sitting outside alone.

Yeah, said the voice, just a bloody animal, driven by hunger and sex.

I am actually a mammoth, said Jay, *only I survived all your ice ages. I may even learn to tango!*

You're talking shit.

You *chose animals. Most people opt for the furry friendliness of the cat family. Or the big-eyed cutesy seals. Or the lean-flanked wild and free horse. Or the do-probe-me inaccessibility of a porcupine. Jamie has no demons like you and defies you with being a skunk.*

Repulsive to humanity and most of the animal kingdom, but irresistible to another skunk! Someday I may meet another mammoth.

The voice went silent.

But Jay continued.

She had been herself, until St Patrick's Day and In Love. More or less fancied herself as a fox, the largest predator in the British Isles, beautiful pelt, amber eyes, full and gorgeous tail; a stink to drive away the timid. Sexy, sexy, sexy. And under the green hypnotic gaze of Lucy, a suspicious wild cat, sheathing its claws and desiring a hearth, a heart.

Chameleon, ever eager to fit in? Selling out?

Jay would have sold her grandmother (if she'd had one) for Lucy's approval. House cat? Puppy? Anything to have Lucy scoop her up from her scrubbed doorstep.

You'll never keep it up! the voice was back with all it could muster as vengeance.

Just watch it, said Jay, sipping brandy, breathing fire, *I may just stomp you with my hairy great mammoth foot.*

Just wait till you fall In Love again!

Oh, it's threat time, is it? Jay closed her eyes and concentrated.

Fee Fi Fo Fum – I'm Not In Love With Anyone!

And now, she thought in the blessed silence, my dear Jay, what would *you* like to do?

The woman next door came and sat beside her. Jay descended from the heights of near madness to wish her a warm good evening.

Armagnac on the terrace? How charming! I like that!

I missed you today, said the woman. *I played the Elvira Madigan Mozart, you would have liked it.*

I do, said Jay. *Very much.*

Well, let's hear it now, said the woman.

They went upstairs.

The woman's room was bare as Jay's. So Jay drifted next door for her dregs of brandy. And the woman — whose name, it happened, was Aurora — whittered on about an infidelity performed against her by a titled husband, an imminent divorce, a Sunday paper scandal.

'Mm,' said Jay, immersed in Mozart.

'None of which has any relevance to you,' said the woman, 'but it's nice and polite of you to listen.'

Jay was waiting for the soul-inspired *Adagio*. Aurora re-filled their glasses, brushed Jay's hand rather unnecessarily as she set her glass down.

'So,' said Aurora, 'what brings you here?'

Suddenly, a long-held bubble of laughter hurtled through Jay as the immaculate second movement started. She sipped brandy, held it on her tongue, set herself alight. She knew her animal, all at once, no question: not cutesy, not brave, not magnificent. Just solid and misunderstood. Welcome home, mammoth, home to a real fire.

'What brings *you* here?' said Aurora again, breathily, as if it mattered, flicking out the light and sitting again with practised gaucherie.

Jay sat back in her chair. She looked at Aurora.

'Honey,' she said, with a real slow smile, 'Honey, don't let me *commence!*